ONCE UPON A BROKEN SKY

M.T. DeSantis

This is a work of fiction. Names, characters, businesses, places, events and incidents are either the products of the author's imagination or used in a fictitious manner. Any resemblance to actual persons, living or dead, or actual events is purely coincidence.

Editing by Stardust Book Services in collaboration with Nastasia Bishop

Cover design by Stardust Book Services in collaboration with Zoe Mellors

Formatting by Stardust Book Services in collaboration with Rae Davennor

To my Twitter Worms (wiggle, wiggle). You rock, and you inspired Zelandra's critical moment.

Zelandra

Zelandra shivered as the rightness settled in her bones. It was a good shiver—always a good shiver. Never the kind she felt … before.

In the mirror over the vanity, Zelandra's reflection showed the smile this shiver always brought. She beamed like the sun once had in her sky. The circus had stopped.

"Finally." She twirled a lock of her floor-length golden hair around one finger. With a thought, ebony-colored ropes sprouted from two of her fingers. They wove into a braid with the golden tresses. Dark, light, dark, light—much like her. She was the favored one, the chosen treasure. Her darkness stood in a place of light.

Two knocks came at the door. In place of the third that

always followed, the door swung wide.

"Zelandra!" Ori bounced into the room. Her jade frock bubbled in rippling waves, and her honey-blonde hair shimmered with silver specks. Its ends curved up to match the broad smile stretching across her youthful face. "Zelandra! We're here! We're here! The performance is so near!"

Zelandra couldn't help a chuckle. Ori's rhymes never failed. "I know. I can feel it." She drew in a deep breath, let it loose on a long exhale. The air filled her with purpose. The purpose filled her with joy. Freedom. True freedom for so many shows now. She would never give up this life.

"It appears I'm not the first one here." Cindell's deep voice preceded her entrance. She stepped through the open door of Zelandra's chamber. Her azure gown shone like a daytime sky.

Daytime. She remembered that.

"Not first, not first." Ori hopped in a circle. The silver dots in her hair winked when her feet left the floor. "To be first, I do thirst. Make the audience burst. Tonight!"

Cindell tried and failed to bite down on a grin. "I think she's a little excited."

"Just a touch," Zelandra said. Though, she could hardly blame Ori for her uncontrollable eagerness. "Are you ready?" She directed the question to Cindell.

The azure mistress straightened so her forehead practically pointed skyward. Bianca always said the top of Cindell's head mingled with clouds. Not that Grimmfay had clouds, but Zelandra remembered those, too.

"I am always ready," Cindell said.

"Ah, we are all here." Bianca swept through the open door. The bodice of her crimson gown hugged her torso above a skirt that billowed in a regal arc. She closed the door with a soft click and approached the mirror-topped vanity. "Let us see what awaits us this eventide." From somewhere in her skirt, Bianca extracted a knife no bigger than her thumb. She punctured the tip of her finger with the tiny blade and pressed the welling bead of blood to the glass. The surface darkened to ebony so the mirror was barely distinguishable from the wall behind it. From the surface's center, circles of crimson, azure, and jade started small and expanded outward, growing and disappearing beyond the mirror's edge in ever faster movements. After several moments, the circles faded, replaced by a simple cottage surrounded by trees.

"Ooh, cute." Ori leaned toward the mirror, her nose almost touching the glass. "Who does such a house suit?"

Cindell gripped Ori's shoulders and pulled her back. "Watch, and we will find out."

In the mirror, a breeze ruffled the leaves. Zelandra imagined the rustling sound they made, the earthy scent of dirt and moss and bark. They were things she knew once but left in a life she no longer needed. There was movement in the cottage, and then the front door burst open. A young girl, maybe eight or nine years, darted outside on stubby legs, her long brown hair bouncing with her jerky motion. Behind her came an older boy, ten or eleven. His hair was the same shade, but his movements were more fluid. He caught the girl around the waist and twirled her off the ground. Her mouth opened wide with silent laughter as she kicked her little feet.

"Children," Bianca said in a tone implying the image had her interest.

"Siblings." Cindell's voice held something darker, almost threatening.

The girl wrestled loose of her brother's hold and fell in a heap. In a flash, she was up and dashing into the trees. The boy followed, his eyes sparkling with youthful fun and ignorance. The children disappeared into the woods, and the image faded to once again show Zelandra's chamber.

"Little ones!" Ori clapped her hands. Her frock shimmied back and forth in a nonexistent wind. "Daughters and sons. I will love them tons and tons."

"Someone should." Cindell's tone still hinted at barely suppressed violence. She shook her head once and straightened. Her face smoothed to passivity, but there was no mistaking the murder in her eyes. "They are what the Master wishes. He will have them."

"Yes." Bianca cleared her throat. "And I … think it best if Zelandra be the one to introduce them to Grimmfay."

Zelandra bit off a sudden breath. Her? A contact for children?"Ori and I may frighten them," Bianca continued. "And you, Cindell—"

"I have no desire to deal with siblings."

Bianca nodded. "As I suspected. Zelandra shall do it."

A low rumble rolled through the floor. Zelandra felt it

through the satin of her slippers as if the slight barrier did not exist between her flesh and the ebony carpet. The rumble meant the Master heard and understood. She watched the mirror for a long moment. When no dark eyes appeared, she released her breath. He heard, understood, and approved. He approved of her being the one to lure children to the circus? How? Why?

"It is decided, then," Bianca said, breaking the silence. "We should prepare. I shall help Zelandra plan.""Yes." Cindell took Ori's wrist and tugged the jade mistress toward the door. "Come, Ori. There is much to do."

"To do, to do," Ori sing-songed as Cindell tugged her from the room. "To in the little ones' ears coo."

When the door closed behind Ori's bouncing form, Zelandra faced Bianca. "What is there to plan? Won't we … I … just offer them everything their life can't give them and wait for them to stay?"

"Yes." Bianca waved one delicate hand toward the door before clasping it with the other. "The plan was a tactic to get Cindell to go. I thought it best if she didn't notice the fear on your face."

Zelandra flinched. So, her trepidation hadn't gone unnoticed. At least it was Bianca who saw. Bianca was the most understanding of the group, the least likely to take rash action or exploit a fear. Not that Cindell would exploit it, but when the azure mistress was angry, all kinds of things were possible.

"I hoped no one would notice." Zelandra sighed and wove the braid of hair and rope around her wrist. "I just wonder if it should really be me. I have no experience with children."

"Nor do I." Bianca shook her head, and her straight black tresses barely moved. "But you have a kinder face than I do. Ori lacks experience, and Cindell has her niece, but ..."

The unspoken words hung in the air like invisible smoke. If it had not been siblings, Cindell might have been the obvious choice. But her own sister and stepsisters had left deep scars. Cindell would sooner kill the children than accept siblings into her confidence, even if they were no blood of hers.

"I know." Zelandra wove an errant lock of hair around her finger. "I just hope I can win their hearts. My own childhood won't help me figure it out."

"Nor would mine." Bianca's voice was small, vulnerable.

Silence fell. Zelandra sought comfort in the slow progression of her hair twirling and pretended not to see Bianca clutch the crimson-colored jewel at her throat. This was why the past needed to remain in the past. Nothing good came from it. No lessons could be learned from those painful times. She had no use for her life before the circus. Neither did Bianca, Cindell, or Ori. The performance offered them freedom, strength—things they never had before. It would be madness to give up such gifts.

"Well." Bianca's voice was its birdlike self once more. "I should finish preparations. Eventide approaches quickly."

"It does." Zelandra let the hair around her wrist unravel and dangle toward the floor. She inhaled a shaky breath. "Have a good performance."

"You as well." Bianca crossed to the door, paused, and glanced back. "You will be all right, Zelandra. I promise."

The words rested, feather-light, atop Zelandra's heart. Where had any such relationship been in the years before the circus? Why had it taken so much pain and suffering to find family? Bianca, Cindell, and Ori had their own troubles, but they were sisters, even if Cindell had never fully come to terms with the idea of sisters.

"Thank you."

Bianca inclined her head then turned and swept from the room.

Alone, Zelandra stared at her reflection for a long time. Physically, she had aged little since joining the circus. Inside, she had grown in ways she never would or could have before. Confidence and power gave her the ability to be a pillar of support, both for herself and for the others. Yes, children unnerved her, but she would do what needed to be done. Bianca and even Cindell, upset as she was, backed her, and Ori showed support in so many little ways only their group understood. Zelandra held up one hand. A delicate length of chain grew from her palm and draped over her wrist. It was amazing, incredible, what she could do, and she would do it for the rest of her life. The world beyond Grimmfay would not have another chance to destroy her. The only way it could was if she chose to let it, and that was a choice she would never make.

Hansten

Something wasn't right.

But he didn't know what it was. Hansten stood in the middle of his bedroom, staring but not really seeing the mess around him. His bed hunkered in the far corner, beneath where the roof slanted down to meet the wall. When he was younger, he'd burrowed in that corner, tossing his wool blanket over his head and snuggling into the tiniest ball he could. He'd been in a cave or a bunny's home—the games of youth. Now, at age eleven, youth was behind him.

At least, it should have been. He would be head of his own house one day, but heads of houses didn't have messy rooms. They didn't stand at the center of chaos and wonder why they felt so unsettled. Grown-ups didn't feel unsettled. They took charge and comforted those around them. They protected and provided. They made their beds and straightened the clothes spilling out of the chest of drawers their parents made and passed down to their children. They swept their own floors and got excited about taking their sisters to the circus.

A shiver ran up Hansten's spine. The circus. Every time he thought of it, something settled wrong in his heart. It was like part of him didn't want to go, which was ridiculous. Circuses were fun, a treat. Besides, Grenna was so excited. He couldn't let her down.

A rapid burst of knocks came at the door. "Hansten!" Grenna. "Are you in there? Come on! It's time!" The door opened, and Grenna bounced into the room on her chubby legs. At age nine, she hadn't quite outgrown her baby fat. Her brown eyes glittered with some internal light, which dulled as she glanced around. "You haven't cleaned up yet?" Her pink lips formed a pout. "But it's time to go."

"I know," Hansten said. Grenna's presence broke the spell of silence and stillness. He ruffled her hair and toed his best pair of hunting boots farther into their corner. He wanted to stay and clean. He wanted to polish every inch of space until the room shined. Something stopped him. Somehow, organizing when he felt so scattered felt wrong. Besides, there wasn't time. "I'll clean when we get back. Ready to go?"

"Ready?" Grenna clapped her hands and hopped in place on one foot. "I was ready hours ago. Let's go!" She grabbed Hansten's hand and tugged him through the door.

Hansten let her lead, glancing back once to frown at the mess. He would clean later, when he felt better. It was probably just the anticipation of the circus making him reluctant. They'd go, come home. He'd clean. Everything would be fine.

Grenna raced down the stairs, forcing Hansten to concentrate on where he put his feet, rather than his messy room. Things like safety didn't cross Grenna's mind when she was excited. If they fell down the stairs and broke bones, they couldn't go to the circus, but that fear didn't slow her. Fear didn't ever seem to affect her. Had he been so careless two years ago? Did crossing the invisible barrier between single and double-digit age change him so much? He put the thoughts on hold as Grenna tugged him through the open kitchen door. She skidded to a halt, and only then did Hansten notice the absence of their pounding footsteps.

"Mom! It's time. We're finally going!" Grenna squeezed Hansten's hand.

Their mother turned from the counter, where she kneaded dough. The scents of honey and ginger permeated the air. There would be lebkuchen when they returned, and Hansten's mouth watered.

"All right." Their mother smiled and waved one flour-covered hand toward the front of the house. "Have fun. Stay together, and—"

"Come home as soon as eventide ends." Grenna finished the list of requirements their parents set out in exchange for letting Grenna and Hansten go to the circus without them. Eventide's night lasted the length of three days—the longest they'd be away alone and a big step for all of them. "We know." She released Hansten's hand to throw her arms around their mother. "See you in a few days."

Their mother returned Grenna's embrace and then hugged Hansten. She rested a hand on his shoulder, which was almost level with hers. "Watch out for your sister."

"Of course." Hansten puffed out his chest and straightened his shoulders. Heads of houses took care of people.

"We'll be fine." Grenna snatched Hansten's hand and pulled him toward the front door. "Come on! We can't miss the opening!"

Again, Hansten glanced back. His mother gave him a wink, shook her head with a smile, and turned back to the dough. Her unconcerned air should have put Hansten at ease. It didn't. Try as he might, he couldn't dismiss the nagging feeling in his gut.

Outside, fresh air blew through the trees. The heavy aroma of wildflowers mingled with the petunias and daisies their father planted last season. The result was a perfume of home smells that brought Hansten some comfort. Grenna's iron grip on his hand suddenly felt reassuring rather than like she pulled him to their doom. Everything would be fine. It was a circus. A place of fun and laughter and amazement. They'd been talking about it for weeks, watching its welcoming lights in the night sky for days, huddled on Grenna's bed and staring out her westward-facing window. A kind of fever had overtaken Grenna every night. It was the most excited Hansten had ever seen her, and who was he to take that away? It was a circus. They'd go, have fun, come home as soon as eventide ended. What could go wrong?

Grenna

Grenna bounced on her toes, making her hair bounce against her back and her shoulders bounce in time with her hair. Her whole body bounced. Shook, really. It was like some kind of energy hummed through her blood and over her skin. The anxious murmurs and shouts of people waiting to enter the show buzzed in her ears. After so long waiting, she was finally here! The circus was right in front of her. Its colorful lights wove through the air above her. Blues and greens ducked and spun around orange and red. The darkest violet hopped along a line of silver, making little arches in the sky. It was amazing. Magnificent! That was the new word she learned this week—magnificent. It was on the circus's poster, and she'd made Mother tell her what it meant over and over again. Strikingly beautiful—so beautiful it struck the mind and heart. Those words repeated themselves in Grenna's head. So beautiful it struck the mind and heart.

"Grenna." Hansten placed his warm hands to either side of her face and turned her head to the left. To the side of the gate, a line of gold stretched up from the ground. It cut through the dance of the other colors to form a star above the center of the gate.

Grenna stared, unable to look away. The star glimmered like the ones in the sky, but brighter—so much brighter. *What do you wish?* it seemed to ask her.

Grenna had heard so many stories of royalty and peasants wishing on stars and having their dreams come true. They were in the books her father brought home from the market, in the tales her mother made up when they had no new books in the house. Stars had power. Stars made things happen. They made wishes real. If it could work in stories, why couldn't it work for her?

"I wish the circus is as magnificent as the word says it should be." Grenna spoke the words with all her heart.

The star winked.

Grenna's heart fluttered. Did the star wink at her wish? Or did it just wink because it was supposed to wink? No, it was her wish. She just knew it.

A quiet settled over the night. Behind the glowing star, the shifting colors stilled and faded. The star, too, disappeared after another moment of watching Grenna. Above, the sky dimmed. Darkest blue turned to black. The stars—the regular stars, not her star—shifted from whitish-silver to blue. The full moon darkened until it shone like a circle of blood, like the blood from the gash she'd gotten playing a few weeks ago. The whisper of a breeze tingled against her legs, and in a moment, the grass came alive, so green it practically glowed.

Grenna sucked in a breath.

Boom!

From somewhere within the circus, arcs of color rose and exploded in the sky. Mighty instruments trumpeted joy and excitement and beginnings into the air. Grenna barely heard her own gasp amidst the booms and other exclamations of awe. The colored explosions formed dust clouds that rearranged into letters.

G. And an R. An I and two Ms. F. A. Y.

"Grimmfay," Grenna mouthed. The word expanded across the sky, so big. It went forever and ever—so much like she hoped the circus would.

The letters flashed white. With another boom, they broke into glittering drops of light that funneled together to form a multi-colored key, which drifted downward on a breeze Grenna couldn't feel. The key fit into the gate's lock with a giant click.

The gates opened.

Open—they were open!

"It's time! Come on!" Grenna grabbed Hansten's hand and yanked him toward the gates. People crowded and pushed, but they wouldn't, couldn't, keep her away. She ducked and swerved through gaps in the crowd, holes where only someone her size could fit through. The silver barrier circling the circus passed overhead, and then she was inside.

Colors. Sound—haunting and enchanting music. And the smell. Something sweeter than chocolate but warmer than newly baked bread and fresher than the berries she picked in the clearing behind her house. She could almost taste the confection those smells would make, feel its gooey goodness on her tongue.

"Grenna?" Hansten's concerned voice came at her ear. He nudged her shoulder. "What's wrong? Are you okay?"

Only then did Grenna realize she'd stopped. The crowd parted around her like a stream splitting for a rock. No one gave her mean looks like they would at lines in the nearby town square. No one cared about the little girl and her brother who'd stopped in the middle of the circus's only entrance. Everyone went on their way, brilliant smiles on their faces, eyes wide.

"It's magnificent." Strikingly beautiful. There was no other way to describe it. Her mother was right. The circus's poster was right. Paths between tents of cherry red and blueberry purple with stripes of sugar-white and the brown-orange of ginger twisted away to places unknown. Grenna wanted to know them. She wanted to see them all, learn all their secrets.

"Grenna?" Hansten's voice was even more concerned.

"We're here." She faced him and gripped both his hands. "We're really here." Off to the right, a sign for dancing swans shimmered white and gold. She pointed to it. "Dancing swans—come on!" She skipped toward the sign, Hansten's hand still in hers. Dancing swans, and then on to the next thing, and the next. She would see everything—everything—the circus had to offer.

Zelandra

Zelandra finished the hundredth stroke of the brush through her hair. She hadn't come close to all of it, but the circus aided its own. A hundred strokes of the brush worked its magic through her trailing locks so they fell around her in a perfect waterfall of golden ringlets. With great care, she set the brush on her vanity and studied her reflection. A quick swipe of pink across her lips and over her eyelids made her ready. She reached for the place where bonds waited. A chain rose to the call. She gripped one end tight and sent the other hurtling into darkness. Tiny jingling sounds filled her chamber. In the distance, there was a clink as it locked in place, and then the ebony walls disappeared. Zelandra shot through shadows, her chain pulling, pulling, until she was suddenly high above a tent filling with spectators. Excited and curious murmurs drifted up from benches facing an empty performance ring. This far away, individual words were lost, but the energy of audience anticipation brought the air to life.

She couldn't wait for their eyes to light up. Zelandra sat on the bench lined with ebony silk and adjusted her gown. The journey never rumpled it or disturbed a strand of her hair. But it didn't hurt to make sure.

Long minutes passed in stillness. The murmur from below grew louder as more people entered the space. On the outside, the tent shimmered the gold of her hair and gleamed the ebony of her sky. Inside, a forest clearing awaited those who entered.

"Guests. Children and children at heart." The circus's disembodied announcer's voice came from nowhere and everywhere. The murmurs cut to silence as if snuffed. "Welcome to The Heights."

Directly below in the performance ring, golden light flashed. A few shrieks came from the audience. The light cleared, revealing a base of ivory stone. Percussive music like masons' tools started, and a choir of birds accompanied the sound. Though she'd seen it countless times, Zelandra watched the structure below start to grow like a tower building itself. She didn't need to—the circus would never let her forget a cue—but something about watching the process filled her with grim satisfaction. A tower had once been her prison, but no such walls would hold her ever again. Layers of ivory were added to the structure. An inch, and then a foot, two feet. Up and up it went. Gasps came from the audience. Zelandra pulled her attention from the show to scan those who came to see her magnificence. They watched the self-building tower with awe and disbelief and perhaps a twinge of fear. So many sets of eyes, all fixated on what lay before. Not what waited above.

All but one.

Zelandra flinched and brought her hands to her face. No—it couldn't be. All watched the tower, except she could have sworn she saw …

Forcing herself to breathe normally, she glanced down again. Sure enough, all eyes were fixed on the show, all but one set peering from beneath thick brown hair. Those, full of warmth and wonder, looked straight up at her.

Zelandra stared. The building sounds faintly buzzed at the back of her awareness. It was impossible. No one should know she was here. No one should yet be able to see her. But this man … he not only saw her, he watched. She met his gaze, and something like lightning sizzled in her blood. He liked what he saw. She transfixed him, commanded his attention. Normally, she would have preened under such appraisal, put on a show to draw his attention, erupted in chains and ropes to ensnare his will and mind. But here, now—all she could do was watch him, too. This man was surrounded by hundreds of people, and yet, they were alone. She wanted nothing more than his eyes on her, not for what she could do, but for herself alone. His gaze roved over her face, her body. Its intensity felt like hands caressing bare skin, and she shivered. His eyes locked with hers again, and something inside her crumbled under the desire in their depths. Never since coming to the circus had she sought the company of a guest. Never had there been the desire. But tonight, the desire took hold and would not let go. She would find him. She would know who he was, how he saw her when none should have had the power. When her performance ended, he would be her goal.

Hansten

Hansten followed Grenna into the tent of sunlight gold and nighttime sky. The Heights didn't tell much as titles went, but the tent's colors had caught Grenna's attention and refused to let go. She had to see what was inside, and as the only thing standing between losing his sister in the crowd and making sure they both got home, he had to follow.

"The gold is so bright—just like the sun!" Grenna repeated for the third or fourth time. "And the dark, the same color as the sky …"

Hansten only smiled and let her haul him through the open flap of the tent that was, truthfully, very similar to the gold of the sun and a match for the circus's nighttime sky. Around them, the bustle of people having excited conversations filled the air, sweeping Hansten up in their joy. So many people having so much fun. He crossed into the tent, and Grenna drew up short with a gasp.

Hansten blinked back to reality and let out a gasp of his own. Inside, the tent wasn't gold and black. Rather, its walls were an intricate mural of a forest. But mural wasn't the right word. The walls were only images, but they were real enough to come alive at any moment. Leaves seemed to rustle in the trees. A deer peered out from between two trunks, its wide eyes fixing on him before it flitted away. Above, a bird's nest rested on a branch, and Hansten could have sworn the tiny chirps of newly hatched chicks came from inside. Up ahead, some kind of illusion made it appear the trees crowded in on the audience space—trunks sticking out and branches descending from the ceiling to give the appearance of thicker growth opening into a sunlit clearing beyond. The speckled pattern of sunlight through leaves dappling the grass looked so real, and a single white boulder sat partially covered by shrubs.

"It's … so real," Grenna said, voice breathy.

Hansten had to agree. He'd lived his entire life at the edge of a forest, spent so many afternoons exploring the trees. Yet if it wasn't for the crowds and benches that made it clear they were at the circus, he could almost believe he was outside. Even the air smelled fresh.

"We have to get closer." Grenna lunged forward, pulling Hansten down the aisle between rows of benches packed with guests. Hansten swerved around a family and ducked under an extended arm just in time to prevent a collision. At the very front of the benches, a railing of vine separated the audience space from the performance ring. Several children already stood against the barrier, and Grenna squeezed into a space just wide enough for her and Hansten.

She bounced on her toes. "I can't wait!"

"Guests. Children and children at heart." The voice that had announced other shows reverberated from everywhere in answer to Grenna's excitement. "Welcome to The Heights."

Applause and cheers followed, quickly quieting as the sunlight pattern on the grass of the clearing began to change. It shivered as if the leaves above moved in a gentle breeze, but there was no wind. A bird trilled. Another responded. The two sang together, holding a warbling note. The note ended. There was a beat of silent stillness. And then a chorus of birds chirped their joy to a tune that was more than bird noises but not quite a melody. The sun patterns on the grass flickered in time to the not-quite-song, creating a dazzling light show.

"Ooh, pretty," Grenna whispered.

It was pretty. The lights flickered and danced. There was no breeze, which made no sense, but Hansten forced himself not to think about it too much. The sounds and sights were realer than real, and trying to figure out how the circus did it was making his head hurt.

The branches and shrubs began a rhythmic swaying. Almost at once, they all leaned slightly away from the center of the ring.

Then, nearly together, they resumed their original places. Their movements changed the light pattern along the grass and grew and grew until the shrubs pressed flat against the ground before straightening. Somewhere amid it all, the birdsong had resolved into a more noticeable melody. Definitely as one, the greenery leaned away from the center, and suddenly, Hansten saw the pearly white boulder for what it was. It rose past the shrubs and branches, up and up and up, seeming to build itself as it went. It wasn't a rock. It was a wall.

"It's a tower!" Grenna squeezed his hand. "An ivory tower. Like in the storybooks." She tilted her head back, her body following, and gasped in time with the rest of the audience. "She's … beautiful …"

Who was? Hansten followed Grenna's gaze, and the breath left his lungs. High above, far higher than the tent should have allowed, a young woman with the longest, most golden, most curly hair stood atop the tower. Little by little, the tower lowered, bringing the woman into view. She wore a gown the same black as the circus's sky, and green eyes like the first leaves of spring peered from a youthful face. With a flick of her wrist, a rope the same shade of her dress dropped from the tower, falling beside the white wall and stopping with its end just above the ground.

Hansten stared at the rope. How did she do that? She was far away but not so far that he couldn't see she hadn't unhooked the rope from something. It was just there. But before he could ponder it too much, the base of the tower changed. At once, it was the same shade of the rope and the woman's dress.

Another gasp rippled through the audience. Grenna's pressure on his hand increased.

A little at a time, the darkness worked its way up the tower. Ivory became ebony, and the rope faded to blend with the smooth surface. Up and up the color climbed until, too quickly and after more time than it should have taken, the top of the tower matched the woman's gown. She continued her downward progress, but now it was as if she stood on air.

She reached the ground. Around her, the light patterns flickered, but they were different somehow. The angle was not what it had once been.

"It's . . . it's her hair!" Grenna released his hand and crushed him in the most excited embrace. "The light's coming from her hair!"

It was true. The light flickered left, right. One moment, zagging lines crisscrossed the grass. The next, beams shot upward in every direction like a burst of stars come to ground. All of it came from the woman's golden locks. The strands shimmered, seeming to move like a waterfall plunging over a cliff but in slow motion. He had no words to describe what he saw. Then, with a sweep of her hands, ebony rope circled the hem of her dress. It matched the material perfectly, and in the back of his mind, Hansten knew he wouldn't be able to see the rope under any other circumstances. But here, surrounded by whatever magic Grimmfay used, it was clear. Another layer of rope ringed her skirt above the first. Then another and another. They covered her skirt, then the bodice, stopping just beneath her chin. Her green eyes stared at a fixed point, and the intensity in their depths took Hansten's breath away. Then, with a flash of darkness—however such a thing was possible—the room dimmed, lightened. And the woman was gone.

"Wow!" Grenna released him to applaud, jumping up and down with an excitement she'd never shown for anything, and she showed excitement for everything. The rest of the audience mimicked her elation, leaving Hansten to feel like a stone caught within a whirling pool.It shouldn't have been possible. Yet, it had happened. The tower changed color, and the woman's hair gave off its own light, and then she disappeared. It shouldn't have been possible.

Why not? A little voice in the back of his head posed the question. *The circus is magic, after all. Why shouldn't anything be possible?*

It was a good question, and Hansten had no good answer. Why not, indeed? Just because he'd never seen it before didn't mean it couldn't be real. Slowly, he brought his hands together so he joined the audience in their cheers. Faster and then a little faster he applauded. Of course it was real. The circus wasn't the everyday forest where he lived. Amazing things could happen here. He whistled his appreciation, his enjoyment, no, his amazement. He clapped in earnest now. Grenna grinned at him. He grinned back. The circus was fantastic, and he would see it all.

Zelandra

The children were in the audience.

But so was … he.

Zelandra stood in the darkness behind the performance ring, one hand pressed to her frantically beating heart. On the other side of the thick fabric, the applause and cheers went on and on. She should have ridden their glory, been alight with how she amazed and enthralled them. She wasn't.

He. The man with the bottomless eyes and beautiful face. Every inch of her remained on fire from the feeling like the power of four mistresses that had passed between them. It was stronger than her bonds, gripped with more fierceness than Ori's thorns, smoother than Cindell's glass, and her blood. Her blood boiled and froze in ways beyond even Bianca's control.He. It wasn't a name. It was barely an identity. Yet, it filled her with all the knowing and wanting in the world. He had seen her before anyone should have known she was there. He watched her and her alone. He wasn't distracted by the rope or the lights or the tower. He saw only her. His intensity had pulled her in, showing her a world beyond the joy of the circus and the sorrow of what came before. If Cindell or Bianca or Ori had asked her if such a feeling was possible only moments before her performance, she would have giggled. Shaken her head at Cindell, shared a knowing look with Bianca, smoothed sweet Ori's hair and told her no with absolute certainty. Nothing eclipsed the joy of Grimmfay. Nothing could more thoroughly wipe away their pasts than the thrills of performing and power.

"He …"The not-name caressed her lips. It made no sense, but it was so. If Cindell or Bianca or Ori asked her now, she wouldn't know what to say. The place where her bonds rested inside her laid silent and still. They gave her strength under every circumstance, but not here. Here, they offered nothing. Who was he?

Out in the performance tent, the cheers finally quieted. The applause lowered from the consistent boom of thunder to the rattle of steady rain and then a few scattered drops before the storm ended. Excited chatter took its place. Zelandra strained to hear his voice, even though she had no idea what it sounded like. Part of her was sure she would just know. Ridiculous. She couldn't possibly. Still, she listened and grew more and more desperate as the chatter faded. People left. He had probably gone, too. Her heart weighed her down. Goddess …

Zelandra sucked in a breath. She stilled. Her thoughts stilled. Everything stilled.

Yes, everything. Thinking about the Goddess had not triggered the Master's wrath and sent the land to rumbling. Odd—it always had before, no exceptions. She released a breath, and awareness returned. The tent was nearly silent now, a few straggling voices drifting away from the performance ring. A few were the deep voices of men. Perhaps he was one.

Zelandra grasped the heavy curtain with trembling fingers. There was no call for this. By rights, she should have gone to her chambers many moments ago and left the tent and all its visitors behind. She should not peer out to see if he lingered. She knew she should not, but nothing could stop her hand from pulling back the fabric, her body from leaning forward, her eyes from peering through the gap.

The nature scene arrayed before her, its animals and winds dormant now. Beyond, empty benches stretched toward the back of the tent where the last few audience members trickled back into Grimmfay's night. He was not among them. Only a family of three, two men who held hands, and two children—a boy and girl—without chaperones. The family and couple left. The boy held the curtain open for the girl. Zelandra strained to peer through the opening. Perhaps He waited beyond. But the view was lost to her. She released a heavy sigh.

The girl whipped around, her long brown hair flowing in a graceful arc. Her brown eyes found Zelandra and widened. She elbowed the boy's side and pointed. "Look!"

The boy turned, and Zelandra stood frozen to the spot. They

were the children from the mirror, the ones she was meant to be guiding. She'd forgotten about them.

"You were amazing!" The girl rushed back toward the ring, her stubby legs almost moving too fast for her. She stopped at the rope surrounding the ring and bounced in place.

"Grenna." The boy approached and placed a restraining hand on her shoulder. "Come on. We shouldn't bother the performers."

"No, it's all right," Zelandra heard herself say through the fog of disappointment and confusion. Disappointment for not finding the man. Confusion for how she could possibly have forgotten the children. They were her main concern, not men with eyes sweet as honey, strong chins, and …

Enough. Her task stood before her. She would not be distracted anymore. She stepped out from behind the curtain and crossed the performance ring to stand in front of the children. The girl—Grenna—stared up at her, jaw slack.

"Your hair … is it real?" she asked in a breathy voice.

The boy groaned. "Grenna …"

Despite herself, Zelandra smiled. Grenna was cute. "It is." She bent down so she was on Grenna's level and held out a clump of her golden curls. "Would you like to feel it?"

Grenna's eyes somehow widened more. "Hansten, can I?"

The boy, Hansten, studied Zelandra for a long moment. Unlike his sister, his gaze held the kind of suspicion common among those who left Grimmfay before the grand performance. That would need to be dealt with quickly. Zelandra offered her most comforting smile.

He stared for another moment before shrugging and slowly removing his hand from Grenna's shoulder. "I don't see why not."

Like a shot, Grenna's hand whipped forward, stopping a hair's breadth from Zelandra's locks. With the most tender care, she caressed the strands. Wonder filled her face. "How did you get it to grow so long? Mother always cuts mine before it gets to my waist."

The words punched Zelandra in the stomach. Her mother had cut her hair once. If it were up to her, it would never be cut again. "Oh, I have my ways."

Grenna continued to grin up at her, and Zelandra's insides twisted a little. So far, so good, but now what? She could work with Grenna's admiration, but Hansten still eyed her as if she'd morph into a towering beast with claws and fangs at any moment. If she was going to win them both over to Grimmfay, she needed them to see the wonder of the circus.

Oh, that was it! She'd show them the wonder. Technically speaking, the mistresses weren't supposed to meander the paths alongside guests, but the Master would understand. She was doing it to fulfill his wishes. She leaned closer to Grenna and lowered her voice to a conspiratorial whisper. "My hair isn't the only amazing thing about the circus, you know."

"Oh, I know!" Grenna hopped up and down. "Your performance was fantastic, and there were the prettiest swans, and the tiny fliers were wonderful!"

Ah, fairies. Ori's show with her fairies started soon. It would mesmerize Grenna and give Zelandra some backup. It seemed like she'd need it. "Do you want to see more fairies?"

Grenna squealed. If her eyes got any wider, they would pop out of her head. "There's more?"

"Grenna." Hansten returned the restraining hand to her shoulder. "I told you, they weren't real. It was an illusion or a trick."

"No, it wasn't." Grenna planted her little hands on her hips and glared up at her brother. "They were real, and I want to see more." She turned back to Zelandra. "Will you show me the other fairies? Please, please?"

"Grenna, no." Hansten stepped closer. "We've already taken enough of … umm."

"Zelandra," Zelandra said, "and you haven't taken up my time at all. I have plenty before my next performance. I'd love to show you the fairies and anything else you want to see."

"There, see." Grenna folded her arms. "Zelandra doesn't mind. Stop being such a downer, Hansten."

The tent fell silent. Grenna glared at her brother. Hansten frowned. Zelandra waited, the knot in her stomach tightening with every moment no one moved or spoke. Hansten was considering. That was good, but if he ultimately refused, she wasn't sure what to do next. Why had everyone thought she was the one to do this? Bianca or even Cindell with her hatred of siblings would have done so much better.

Finally, Hansten exhaled. "All right."

"Wonderful!" Zelandra grinned. The knot in her stomach loosened but didn't unravel completely. She definitely had her work cut out for her. She extended her arm, palm open, toward the flap at the back of the tent. "Then, let's see Grimmfay."

Grenna

They were going to see fairies!

Grenna skipped along, her little hand tucked firmly in Zelandra's grasp. Every tent they passed shone brighter than the last. Zelandra seemed to know what Grenna was thinking. She'd point out signs or shows and describe them before Grenna could ask. Her words mingled with the circus's lullaby-like music, but rather than putting her to sleep, the combination woke Grenna up like she'd never been awake before. Mice who wore suits and gowns, pigs who juggled, fox cubs who made pyramids—magic was everywhere!

"Would you care for something to eat?" Zelandra pointed to a window that seemed to hover in midair.

"Ooh, yes." Grenna squinted at the curly writing over the window. "Concens?"

"Concessions," Hansten said. "It's a big, fancy word for snacks."

She loved snacks. "What do they have?"

"Whatever you'd like." Zelandra tugged her to the window. "Popped corn, fried dough, brownies—"

"Wait," Hansten said. "How much does this cost? Mom and Dad didn't give us money for lots of treats."

Zelandra offered a soft smile. "No charge for special guests."

Grenna's excitement ballooned like a bubble in her chest. All-she-could-eat snacks? The circus really was the best place in the world.

"Ah, guests." A girl with orange hair and fox ears grinned from the other side of the window. "What can I get you?" She reached up with one hand—almost a paw—and unfurled a scroll Grenna sworn hadn't been there a moment ago.

More curvy writing listed out offerings—sticky buns, brownies, cookies—so many choices! How could she pick just one?

"Nothing for me," Hansten said. He stood a step or two behind Zelandra with his arms folded.

He was no fun. Grenna studied the list again. "They all look so good. Oh ... the caramel brownie, please."

The fox-girl winked. "Coming right up." She rolled up the scroll and reached beneath the window before revealing a caramel brownie on a blue napkin. "Enjoy."

Grenna took the treat and crammed a bite in her mouth. Sweetness and gooey goodness coated her tongue. It was the best brownie she'd ever had—even better than grandma's. "So good," she said through a mouthful. "Where do the desserts come from?"

Zelandra shook her head with a smile. "I'm afraid I don't know, but we should hurry. We don't want to miss the fairies."

Grenna took another bite and followed Zelandra down a path. How could Zelandra not know where the brownies came from? Maybe the circus got them from an outside source? But even as she thought it, she knew it was wrong. The circus kept its magic within its borders, so if Zelandra didn't know who made the brownies, it was likely a secret, which was too bad. She wanted to see where the treats came from and meet the baker who made them.

Up ahead, the row of tents ended at an open area. A woman with white hair and a gray dress sat still as people passed. Though she didn't move at all, there was something almost alive about her. But what?

"A doll?" Hansten's voice was annoyed. "I knew there weren't fairies."

A fire stoked to life in Grenna's belly. She swallowed her bite of brownie and rounded on him. "Just because you don't see them, doesn't mean they aren't there."

Hansten didn't back down. "Grenna, it's a doll on a chair."

"It's more than that." Grenna didn't try to keep the whine out of her voice. Her brother was so irritating. Couldn't he see something was going to happen here?

"Your sister's right," Zelandra said in her calm way. She pointed one delicate finger to the woman Hansten insisted was a doll. "Watch."

"Yeah, watch." Grenna spun away to face the woman. Her shoulders heaved with her anger. If Hansten wanted to complain about everything, fine. She could enjoy herself without him. She shoved the remaining brownie in her mouth. The sweetness soothed her, and she waited.

For a few minutes, nothing happened. Then, like when a storm rolled in at home, something in the wind changed. Grenna couldn't explain it, but suddenly, she knew the open area was a performance, not just a place where people went from one attraction to the next.

"Ah, it's starting." Zelandra bent to speak close to Grenna's ear. "Watch carefully."

Grenna stared so hard her eyes felt like they might fall out. She wouldn't miss whatever it was Zelandra wanted her to see. A light breeze ruffled her hair and then ruffled the hair of the doll. There was stillness, and then, like magic, three fairies, each clad in a simple green dress, hovered around the doll's head.

Grenna gasped and gripped Zelandra's hand. "Oh …"

Zelandra chuckled. "Watch."

Grenna could do nothing else. The fairies rose above the doll's head and touched wands of moonlight, starlight, and sunlight together. A spark of green light lit where they touched and shot downward toward the doll. The doll's dress turned from gray to green, and the fairies swooped into an acrobatic show, wands turning gray hair to honey-yellow and white flesh to the rosy pink of the icing her mother made for treats on special occasions. Round and round and round the fairies flew until one created a crown of light atop the doll's head.

And then, the doll moved.

This time, Grenna's gasp was lost amid similar sounds from the rest of the crowd. The doll was alive. The doll was a woman, and not just any woman. A princess! The princess gazed around, eyes locking on Grenna. With a grin and a wink, she stood and twirled.

"She's real." Grenna's voice barely reached her own ears. Fairies and a princess. The circus was the most wonderful place she'd ever been. "I … I want to meet her."

Zelandra squeezed Grenna's hand. "That can be arranged."

Zelandra

Grenna was entranced, and Zelandra couldn't believe her luck.

"It's not real," Hansten said, huffing. "She's powered by clockwork or something."

Well, part of her luck. With one sibling ready and willing to run into Grimmfay's embrace, she was far ahead of where she expected to be. She'd brought others into Grimmfay, taken them away from harsh lives to be their best selves. A hollowness settled around her heart as Ori continued her performance. Zelandra had seen it before many times, but even so, it never ceased to amaze her. The way Ori's gown sparkled and her hair shimmered brought life to Grimmfay's night. Jade was such a lively shade. Not like ebony. Ebony promised no flash, nothing of the princess-like quality Ori had. They were so different, yet they came together with the strongest bond, stronger than any Zelandra could conjure.

Ori's twirling grew faster and faster. Against the circus's lilting music, the movement seemed like too much. Though, Zelandra doubted any heard the music but her. Ori stole attention. Even Hansten watched the show, his shoulders alternating between tense and relaxed. Beyond him, people of all types fixed their attention on the dancing princess; a tall woman with hair and skin like Grimmfay's sky, a group of youths stuck in the gangly stage between child and adulthood, a woman with brown hair and a stance like soldiers Zelandra had seen at past performances where royalty was present, and—

Him.

Grenna squeezed Zelandra's hand again, but the feeling was so far away. He was here. Her heart leaped to a gallop. She expected the search to be long and tedious, checking here and there while she kept her attention fixed on Grenna and Hansten. What had Mother always said? When she stopped hunting for something, it appeared—one of the few useful things she ever told her. Zelandra hadn't forgotten about him, but he'd gotten pushed to the back of her mind. And now, here he was, watching Ori's performance.

Except, he wasn't watching Ori's performance. He was staring back at her.

Zelandra inhaled. The world spun. Ori should have commanded everyone's attention. The princess in jade should have hypnotized them all. But not him. He spared no glance for the performance. He saw her—only her, and just as quickly as she inhaled, Zelandra lost her breath. She had to meet him.

In the performance ring, light flashed, signaling Ori's disappearance. Silence fell over the courtyard, and then applause thundered through the air. Grenna released Zelandra's hand to clap and cheer. The man didn't move. Neither did Zelandra, and thoughts came together with lightning clarity. Grenna wanted to meet Ori. Zelandra needed to get away. She tilted her head to the man to tell him she needed a moment. He tilted his toward the brown-haired guard woman and then to a tent of deepest violet. He would meet her there.

Quivering, Zelandra nodded. Grenna still cheered, and Hansten stared at the ground, his shoulders up by his ears. A brief twinge of regret flickered through her before it disappeared like Ori had. She was supposed to introduce the children to Grimmfay. But that didn't mean she had to be the only performer they interacted with. She would pass them to Ori for a bit, slip into the crowd, and meet … him.

Finally, the cheering slowed and stopped. Grenna bounced to stillness. "That was amazing!" She whirled and gripped Zelandra's hand again. "Do you know her? Can we meet her? Please, please?"

Hansten mumbled something that might have been an objection, but he still stood stiff as a wooden board and stared at the ground.

Zelandra spoke before he could regain himself. "I do, and of course you can." She glanced past them to where her handsome stranger stood in conversation with his guard. Ori had teleported into an empty tent a bit beyond him. Zelandra shivered. She would be so close for a moment. She forced herself to smile at Grenna. “If we hurry, we can catch her. This way. I’ll introduce you to Orianna.”

Hansten

Hansten trudged after Zelandra and Grenna. Every step jolted him. The circus offered him every dream he'd had before he was old enough to understand life. He wanted them all, wanted to give in and be a kid forever.

And that wanting terrorized him to his core. The performances were magnificent—too magnificent. They couldn't be real. Magic wasn't real.

Zelandra passed by a regal-looking man and a brown-haired woman, slowing briefly before turning toward a green tent. Even these two adults wore mystified expressions. How? Adults were supposed to be practical. They weren't supposed to believe in fancy or enchantment. He was eleven. He was an adult now, but that knowledge didn't keep him from wanting and wishing at every wondrous thing he saw. Grenna frolicked and skipped without a care in the world. Why couldn't she see? And why could he?

Zelandra stopped outside the green tent, pulling Grenna to a halt. Grenna bounced forward then backward before settling, still vibrating with energy. Zelandra opened the tent flap and stuck her head inside. "Ori, are you there?"

"There?" A sing-song voice came from inside. "There. Where? And everywhere. It's only fair."

Grenna stilled. "It's her." She inhaled the words on a nearly silent breath.

Zelandra stepped aside and held the flap open. "After you."

Grenna disappeared inside, and Hansten rushed after her. Goddess, he could not let Grenna out of his sight. He crashed into something and fell forward, sprawling in a tangle of limbs with—

"Hansten!" Grenna pushed him off her and stood, brushing off her trousers and smoothing her hair. She planted her chubby hands on her hips and glared at him. "Why did you knock me over?"

Hansten's face heated, and he ducked his head to hide any pink visible in the dimness. "I … sorry. I didn't mean to."

"No harm done, little one." The woman—Ori—crossed to him on feather-light steps. She held her hand out, an offering to help him up. "Come."

Hansten didn't move. Accepting help from a performer felt like giving in. But ignoring her hand was rude, something his mother would lecture him about. Reluctantly, he took Ori's hand and let her pull him to standing. When he was upright, he let go with a muttered thanks and brushed off his clothes.

"Of course." Ori beamed. "Not to help brings remorse." She giggled, and silver sparkles erupted over her skirt.

Grenna gasped. "How did you do that?"

"What, these?" Ori spread her skirt and twirled in a haze of silvery green. "With the ease of summer's breeze. Sprinkle, sparkle in the darkle." She frowned, and the silver specks blinked. "Darkle . . ."

Grenna giggled. "I love your rhymes."

Ori perked up, the silver specks dancing a little. "Rhyme is sublime at any time. Never a crime are mine." She spread her skirt again, but this time she lowered into the graceful curtsy of a princess. "Ori, Orianna, is my name? What are thine?"

"Grenna," Grenna said, too eager.

Hansten bit his lip. Ori—Orianna. Ori was her nickname. Zelandra called her that, and Grenna could if she wanted. But he was going to think of her as Orianna. The name felt more distant, easier to push away. "I'm Hansten, soon-to-be head of my own house."

Grenna snorted.

Hansten's cheeks heated again. He whirled on her, mouth open, but Zelandra rested a hand on his shoulder.

"Please, don't fight." She knelt before him. "There's so much to see. Don't lose your time arguing over things that aren't important right this moment."

Hansten drew in a slow breath and let it go. Maybe he was being too harsh. Zelandra was right. The circus only lasted a little while, and hadn't he been so excited to bring Grenna to something she'd looked forward to for weeks? Just because he had a strange feeling didn't mean something was actually wrong. He hadn't even given the circus a chance, only chosen to see how he thought it affected Grenna's judgment. Maybe his sister was right. Maybe he was being no fun. He could try. Trying couldn't hurt.

"You're right." He slipped out from Zelandra's hand and moved to stand in front of Grenna. It took some effort to meet her gaze, but as his father always said, any apology worth making was worth making to someone's face. "I'm sorry for how I've been acting. I'm just ... not myself tonight."

Grenna pursed her lips. Then she smiled and took his hands in her smaller ones. "I forgive you."

"Yay!" Orianna flung her arms wide and spun, the silver specks dancing along her dress. "See, everything's okay. Forgiveness is always the way." She came to a stop and extended an arm toward the tent flap. "Shall we see Grimmfay?"

"Yes!" Grenna hopped once before turning to Hansten with a questioning look.

He opened his mouth, but no sound came. Even with his change of heart a minute ago, something still nagged at him. Something about the circus didn't feel right. Part of him still wanted to pull Grenna close, run for the exit, and never look back. But her eyes shone with such hope and excitement. As her older sibling, it was his responsibility to make sure she was safe, but he also wanted her to have a good time. He couldn't let her down. He forced a smile. "Sounds like fun."

"Good." Zelandra straightened. She appeared thoughtful for

a moment before her eyes brightened. "Ori, do you want to take Hansten and Grenna to see the golden harp? I … need to meet with Bianca, and I'll catch up with you at the performance."

"Ooh, the harp," Orianna sing-songed. "Promises to pluck at your heart."

"What's the golden harp?" Grenna asked.

Orianna winked. "You'll see. But first, I change me." Orianna tugged on her dress, and like magic, the underlayers causing the material to form a bell shape disappeared, leaving only the top green layer. The skirt hung straight and did not sparkle. With a shake of her head, Orianna's vibrant honey-blonde hair dimmed a hue or two—just enough so it didn't stand out so much.

How did she do that?

"How did you do that?" Grenna echoed his question, but her voice held more wonder and much, much less fear than his inner voice.

Orianna smoothed her dress. "Easy-peasy when you know the weasy."

Zelandra laughed, but the sound was a little forced. At least, it seemed to be. "She means it's easy when you know the way. Are you ready now?"

"Oh, yes," Orianna said. "Fixed dress and tress. Out we go to see the rest."

Zelandra backed toward the tent flap. "Then, I'll see you soon." And she was gone.

"Soon, soon. To hear the harp play a tune. We better fly like the moon." She took Grenna's hand and then reached for Hansten's, capturing his fingers between her own, smooth as a child's. "Zoom, zoom, zoom!" She tugged them toward the tent flap.

Grenna jogged at her side. Hansten forced himself not to lag. He still couldn't explain how Orianna made her dress disappear. He couldn't explain so much of the circus. Maybe that was his problem—he searched for explanations where there were none. Grenna was content to just let the magic happen. Since they arrived, he'd scolded her for believing impossible things were real, but there might be something to her view. If he relaxed, Grimmfay might surprise him. He wasn't sure if he could truly let his guard down, but for Grenna, he would try.

Zelandra

Ori and the children skipped off toward the golden harp, and Zelandra almost couldn't believe they went. It had been a moment of genius—sending them in the opposite direction of her meeting place and saying she needed to see Bianca. Her gut twisted at lying to Ori. She almost hadn't been able to go through with it. She knew how much lies hurt and what damage they could do. They were not a habit she wanted to keep, but just this once, for him, she would make an exception.

Ori tugged the children around a corner and out of sight. Zelandra waited another moment to make sure they didn't return, and then she crept from her hiding place, smoothing her skirt. Perspiration coated her palms, and she trembled. In the place below her heart, her bonds grew restless. She crooned to them in her mind, telling them everything would be all right. Though, she wasn't sure if the comfort was for them or her. Across Ori's performance ring, the violet tent waited. With a deep breath, Zelandra started toward it, careful not to bump any of the many guests who milled around her. Two girls, maybe Grenna's age, played at a nearby fish pond. They called for their mother to come see, and two women rushed over. A game of splashing ensued, accompanied by high-pitched laughter. Zelandra smiled, and some of her nervousness eased. Moments like this reminded her why she performed. The circus brought such joy to its guests. She moved on, the laughter echoing in her ears until she reached the violet tent. There, the nerves returned with a vengeance. What if he didn't come? What if she'd taken too long and he got tired of waiting? What if he took one look at her and decided she wasn't worth his time?

And what if she spent so long questioning that she never tried to find him? She wiped her clammy palms on her skirt again and slipped into the tent. Inside, mirrors stretched in every direction and angle, reflecting the room back on itself again and again. Hundreds, maybe thousands, of Zelandras stood still, poised at the beginning of a hundred or a thousand stories—waiting, listening, hoping … searching, finding hundreds, maybe thousands, of … him.

The air stilled. The world stopped. For a moment, there was nothing but her, him, and the openness between them. Then he moved. She moved, stopping close enough to touch. The little distance she dared not yet breech between them echoed hundreds or thousands of times.

"You came." His voice was deep and pleasant and sent tremors through her blood.

"So did you." Her own voice was barely more than a whisper. A second later, she realized how obvious the statement was, and she blushed. "Which you already knew."

He laughed. His laughter, too, was warm and rich and tingle-making. "Then, to be fair, you also knew you were here. So, we're both obvious."

Zelandra couldn't help a grin. Handsome, a calming voice, and a sense of humor. Her shivers ebbed a bit. "Have you been waiting long?"

"Not too long." He gestured behind her. "It took longer than I thought to convince my guard to go sightseeing without me."

His guard? Zelandra remembered the brown-haired woman who carried herself like the kind of protector royalty brought to the circus. "Are you a king?"

He wrinkled his nose. "Prince." He bowed, took her hand between strong fingers, and planted a delicate kiss on its back. "Prince Torrick, at your humble service."

A different type of shiver crested in a wave. His hand was large and strong and warm. It felt … right wrapped around hers. The thought felt like a betrayal. Nothing in her life before Grimmfay had ever felt right. The circus brought all the rightness she needed. So why, then, did he outshine its rightness by so much?

Torrick—such a strong name—frowned. "Are you all right?"

Her cheeks warmed. How many times would she make a fool of herself in front of him? What was wrong with her? She cleared her throat. "Fine, sorry. I'm Zelandra. Mistress Zelandra." Her title came almost as an afterthought. Something strange was happening to her, indeed.

"Mistress?" He shifted his hand so his fingers wove through hers. "What does being a mistress mean, exactly?"

Tingles shot through her, almost stealing her voice. "I ..." She faltered. Yes, she'd spoken despite the new feelings coursing through her, but she had a new problem to go with them. How did she explain her place among the circus? She'd never thought about what being a mistress meant. She, Bianca, Cindell, and Ori just knew it meant holding power and being the most impressive performers in the show. It meant respect and beauty and the strength of their color, but none of these things seemed adequate to explain it to a stranger who had no frame of reference for how Grimmfay worked. How had she never noticed this sooner? Probably because no one had ever asked. But now, someone had, and she needed an answer. "It means being amazing. It means doing the Master's bidding above all else."

Torrick tilted his head. "So, it means being a servant?"

"No." The response shot from Zelandra's lips. He had it all wrong. This was tougher than she thought. How could she explain? "It means being able to do what the Master cannot and making sure it is done exactly how he demands."

Torrick frowned, and a crease appeared between his eyebrows. "That sounds like what servants do for my family. We order a task be done, and they do it, no questions asked."

"It's not the same." But this time, the words didn't come as quickly or with as much ease. When he put it that way, the two did sound very similar. Was she little more than a servant to the Master?

No. She wasn't. She couldn't be. The mistresses were the treasured ones. They were the ones he trusted, the ones with the power to see things done. Hansten and Grenna were destined to be with the circus, and he entrusted their acclimatization to no one but his closest, most powerful performers. It was not like the servants of royalty. She and her sisters did what they did out of loyalty.

But weren't servants to royalty there because they were loyal?

"I think I overstepped." Torrick spoke softly. "I'm sorry. I didn't mean to offend." He started to pull his hand away.

A chill like winter's depths stole through her flesh where they parted. She gripped his hand before it released hers completely. "No, you didn't offend me. I'm sorry. I've … never had anyone ask me these things before."

"So I caught you with your guard down, then." His hand wrapped around hers, returning the warmth. "Let's not mention it again. Your performance was outstanding."

The warmth pulsed and spread down her arm to where her heart fluttered against her ribs. She knew it was outstanding, of course, but to have someone actually say it. The only confirmation she'd ever gotten or needed was the seemingly endless cheers of the audience. But when Torrick said it, the word took on a whole new meaning. "Thank you. Grimmfay has many other outstanding performances. Would you like to see them?" She left off the *with her* but hoped it came across in the subtext. And she thought she was bad with children. This prince was turning her reason to ruin.

"I'd love to." He squeezed her hand.

Subtext received, it appeared. Perhaps she wasn't so bad at this, after all. "Good. Is there anything special you'd like to see?"

Torrick tilted his head and worried at his lip. "Are there any dragons?"

Zelandra blinked. "Dragons?" That wasn't what she'd expected.

"Yes, you know. Roar. Breathing fire. Dragons. Like the kind in storybooks where princes team up with princesses to rescue knights in distress."

She giggled. "I know what dragons are. And, yes, I do believe I have one in mind. Come."

She tugged him toward the tent's flap. He followed without resistance, and a little piece of her soul deep within the place where her bonds lived failed to convince her she made a mistake. Torrick had asked questions she should never consider, not even acknowledge. And now she wandered off with him for a flight of fancy. She was supposed to be winning over Grenna and Hansten to the circus, not frolicking with princes who made unknowing comparisons about her life. But his hand felt so good in hers, and was it her imagination or did the ground glimmer brighter? She opened the violet tent's flap, revealing the world of color and sweetness beyond.

Torrick drew up short and inhaled a slow breath. "It's so pretty from this angle."

Zelandra knew that feeling—the feeling of being awakened to Grimmfay's beauty for the first time. There was nothing like the circus, nothing like the phantasm and wonder it offered. She knew. And soon, Torrick would, too.

"It does." She pulled him out into the air, where the lilting music seemed to croon a song of coming together. "Let me show you Grimmfay."

Grenna

Grenna crammed the last of the cinnamon bun into her mouth and closed her eyes. So sweet! How did Grimmfay do it? The snacks were even better than her mother's, and she'd never had snacks better than mother's.

"Is there a place to … umm?" Hansten held half an uneaten powdered-sugar doughnut. How had he not finished it yet? He gestured around and shrugged. "I need to … nature is calling me." Then his eyes lit up. "Oh, right there. Never mind. Grenna, come on."

Grenna shook her head and pointed to her mouth. "Still eating, and I don't have to go."

Hansten held out the hand not holding the half-eaten

doughnut. "You say that now, but you'll wish you did later."

Why was he being so bossy? "I don't have to go."

"We'll wait right here, dear," Lady Orianna said before Hansten could argue more. "Grenna's with me. You've nothing to fear."

Hansten looked like he didn't quite believe her, but after a minute, he nodded. "Fine. Be right back."

"Hang on." Grenna grabbed his wrist. "Are you going to finish your doughnut?"

Hansten stared at the doughnut as if he'd forgotten he held it. How could he forget about the best sweets in the world? "Umm, no, here." He handed it to Grenna and disappeared into a nearby tent resembling a cottage with fabric patterned like cut logs.

Grenna stuffed the doughnut in her mouth, and the sweetness of powdered sugar coated her tongue. Really, how had Hansten not finished this? How could he think about nature's call with something this good waiting to be eaten? Like the brownie earlier, the cinnamon bun and doughnut just called to her. Kind of like the circus. They wanted her to enjoy everything. She wanted that, too.

"Ooh, a powdered sugar smile!" Ori pointed to Grenna's face and formed her lips into an exaggerated grin. "A new style? Or just eating was worth your while?"

Grenna giggled and started to use her sleeve to wipe the sugar away. What was she doing? If eating was worth her while, she had to finish the treat. She licked her lips until there was no sweetness left. "Delicious!"

Ori's grin reformed into a more normal one. "As is everything here, my dear."

Grenna dusted her hands, and the sugar fell away. Worthwhile or not, licking her fingers felt wrong to do out among people. "I asked Zelandra, but she didn't know. Do you know where the treats are made?"

Ori stilled, and her grin turned to a thoughtful frown. "Hmm. No one has ever asked about the task of making treats and sweets. They just eat. But how they are made, I could not say."

"Oh." Grenna sagged. Ever since she was small, she loved being with her mother and grandma in the kitchen. Seeing yummy confections turn from dough to cookies or cakes filled her heart with warmth. She'd even learned the word confections so she could tell other kids about her family's baking and sound smart. "That's too bad. I wish I could see where they're made."

"Wish?" Ori knelt and took Grenna's hands in her soft ones. Her eyes were intense but still playful somehow. "Wishing is like fishing—you cast a line and reel in what's thine."

Thine? Ori had said the word earlier. It sounded familiar from an old storybook. Something that belonged to someone, maybe was the meaning? Grenna unraveled Ori's rhyme. She'd been fishing with Father a few times. She cast her line into the water and waited, pulling in the fish she wanted. So if wishing was like fishing …

"Do you mean …" Grenna almost couldn't finish the thought. "If I wish it, I could …"

"Fish it." Ori squeezed Grenna's hands. "Wishes bring what we most want. Just wish. Do not let your wish daunt."

Grenna blinked. "Daunt?"

"Do not be afraid." Ori continued as if Grenna hadn't interrupted, but somehow, Grenna knew daunt meant not to fear. "Wishes are meant to be made and come true." She released one of Grenna's hands to tap Grenna's chest right above where her heart beat. "If you wish for you."

Grenna's breathing filled her ears, blocking out the chatter of other guests and even the ever-present music. Ori couldn't be saying what it sounded like she meant. Wishes didn't come true. At least, none of the ones she'd ever made on stars at home had. She gazed up to the sky, the color of Zelandra's gown, and the blue stars twinkling like little bits of day trying to peek through. Wishes on normal stars didn't come true. But what about magic stars—because she was sure these stars were magic? Would a wish on these stars make her dream real? She found one that seemed to gleam brighter than all the rest and offered it all the hope in her heart.

I wish ... I wish ... to see where the treats are made?

"All right. Sorry I took so long." Hansten's voice broke through Grenna's haze. She blinked the star from her vision, and the sounds of the circus returned. Laughter came from somewhere close, and she smiled at the sound of people having fun.

"Not to worry. When needs must, scurry." Ori straightened. "But if we're to see the harp, we best hurry." She took Hansten's hand and pulled them down a path.

Grenna jogged to match Ori's energy. Ori was such an interesting person. She put her whole self into the tiniest movements. Even blinking was a party. Her dress and hair weren't sparkling at the moment, but something about her glittered anyway.

"Here we are. It wasn't far."

Again, Grenna blinked from her thoughts. This time, a tent of the purest gold awaited her. A voice from somewhere called for guests to see the golden harp, the most magical music. Ori led them through the tent flap and into a space filled with benches and people. Ahead, a performance area was empty, except for a beanstalk.

"Beans?" Hansten asked as Ori sat them on a bench toward the front. "I thought we were seeing a harp?"

"The beans are the bait," Ori said and folded her delicate hands in her lap. "Wait."

Bait? Grenna met Hansten's gaze and found her question in his eyes, too. He shrugged. She shrugged back and settled into her spot on the bench. Ori knew what she was talking about. So, they'd wait.

The tent continued to fill, and Grenna tried not to squirm. Was it really taking forever for the show to start, or was she just impatient?

"Artistic guests." Finally! A voice like the music outside drifted from everywhere. "Children of music. Feast your ears upon … The Golden Harp."

The tent hushed. A light from somewhere above shone on the beanstalk, making it glow a bright green almost the same shade as Ori's dress from earlier. The plucking of strings floated on the air. Each note started strong and grew quiet, lingering until the next note overtook it. Where did it come from? Grenna glanced around, but like the voice that announced the show, the source of the sound couldn't be found. Huh, sound, found—she was rhyming like Ori.

The notes continued at their steady pace, forming a melody both familiar and new. Grenna got swept up in their song, and the performance ring faded to be replaced by the woods out near her house. A lazy wind rustled the leaves of the trees where chipmunks and squirrels lounged, chittering in dialogues a little too quiet to hear. Birds glided from twig to twig, silently greeting one another. In the grass, bunnies hopped and played, their little feet making no sound. The only noise was the harp's melodic tune painting the perfect spring day. The blue sky, indeed similar to Grimmfay's stars, peeked through the trees. Glittering golden sunlight cast its beams, each in time with a new pluck of the harp's strings.

Grenna went still, barely able to breathe. How did the harp know? The idea seemed silly. Harps didn't think. They couldn't know anything. But this one felt like it did. This harp took these images from her mind somehow and made them feel real. The whole circus did that—took everything Grenna wanted and made it real.

Realer than real.

The string's pattern changed. Sun beams struck slightly faster but still in a lazy way. Everywhere they hit, something changed. The squirrels and chipmunks left their poses and scurried down the trunks of their trees. Birds settled in nests. Bunnies hopped into burrows. The entire scene rose, and Grenna tilted her neck back to follow it. Up and up and up—like Zelandra's tower. But instead of a maiden, the forest faded, and in its place was …

A harp of gold that played by itself.

Grenna gasped and then gasped again when she heard herself breathe. Around her, all kinds of sounds joined the harp's tune. Gasps were some, and amazed cries, questioning murmurs.

"What?" Hansten's disbelieving voice.

The harp's song changed again, growing slower. The notes were haunting now. They called to the sad place in Grenna's heart that recognized Grimmfay would be gone when eventide ended.

Gone. The thought stopped her in her tracks. Gone. She'd known it all along, but somehow with the harp's song plucking at her heart, it felt too true. Tears sprang to her eyes. She didn't want the circus to leave. She didn't want to leave the circus. She'd only been here a short time, but it already felt like a second home in so many ways. Zelandra was so kind. And Ori with her rhymes and childlike joy. She was a grown-up, but she acted like she was a kid, and it made Grenna feel less bad about wanting to be excited about everything. At home, she'd have to give up her excitement. She'd have to grow up, meet someone, build a house, work, cook, care for children. The thoughts spiraled one after another until her heart raced. She didn't want those things. She didn't want to have the fun removed from her world. She wanted to bake treats and listen to music and see the faces of other children light up as they saw the circus for the first time. She wanted to make the treats, not just know where they came from, and she wished Grimmfay would never end.

The light illuminating the beanstalk winked out. Grenna blinked and realized all was silent. The show ended, and she missed it. "What happened?" Her voice rasped. "Where's the harp?"

"All done," Ori said. She sniffed as if she'd been crying a little, but her eyes were dry. "And now back to the fun."

"Grenna?" Hansten rested a hand on her knee. It sounded like he'd been crying, too, and his eyes glistened with unshed tears. "Are you all right? That was …"

"I'm okay." Grenna gripped her brother's hand. Her heart ached for them, for him. Had he experienced the same sorrow and desire she had? Why hadn't Ori or Zelandra warned them? But even as she wondered, she understood why. The harp's song was personal. There was no warning, and it needed to work its magic how it did. Unlike other shows, it wasn't about pretty things or amazing feats. The harp showed her what was in her heart.

"Odd." Ori's voice was far away. "Where has she trod?"

Trod? Grenna forced herself to focus on the world around her. "Who? What?"

"Zelandra." Ori frowned. The sorrow was gone from her face. "She said she'd meet us here, but she is nowhere near."

"You're right," Hansten said after a minute. "Maybe she's still meeting with … what was her name?"

"Bianca." Ori stood quickly and took Grenna's free hand. "Maybe. Let's go see."

Hansten stood and tugged Grenna up. She let him, but her mind remained behind with the harp and its message. Grimmfay needed her. It needed someone to bake and make treats and give guests sweets. It needed a place where children and children-at-heart could see the confections being made. The crowd pressed in around her, but Grenna didn't feel their closeness. She saw it now—a little cottage made of candy and chocolate, where she could bake and bake until she finished and then bake some more.

No work. No children to care for. Just all the children who came to the show. She could make them all happy, just like the idea of staying and baking made her insides feel gooey like honey.

Hansten tightened his hold on her hand. And of course, Hansten! They could bake together. She'd always been the best at mixing and decorating, but he could be her loyal assistant, putting unbaked cakes and cookies into the oven and taking them out when they became treasures. They could stay like kids together, forever laughing and smiling and puffing flour at one another. She squeezed his hand and let herself come back to reality. After they found Zelandra, Grenna would ask about staying. She'd describe it so perfectly, and Hansten wouldn't argue. He'd love the idea, and they'd be together. Forever.

Zelandra

Grimmfay was amazing. Of course, she'd known this for as long as she'd been there, but not since the very first performance had she really seen the circus's glory. Everywhere, people smiled. Tents dazzled beneath her ebony sky. Cindell's stars gleamed, and Bianca's moon cast an ethereal glow over it all. Below her feet, Ori's grass shone with its own kind of light, and it was so soft against the bare skin where Zelandra's foot met her satin slippers.

"Which way?" Torrick's voice came close to Zelandra's ear.

She flushed and blinked out of her thoughts. "Left. Not far now." And she was sure the handsome man at her side had everything to do with her new view. The way he held her hand, as if letting go would mean losing the very air he breathed—it made everything brighter somehow.

She wove around the audience for the fox cubs and entered a tent of earthy brown. Inside, the tent offered the feel of being in a tunnel, an illusion, if a well-crafted one. A performance ring at the tent's center showed only a tall, narrow stone. Zelandra brought Torrick to a bench three rows back and sat on the aisle.

"Should we sit closer?" he asked, gesturing to the empty benches.

Zelandra shook her head. "It's a little-known secret that the third row offers the best view."

"Hmm." Torrick scooted closer so his body pressed against hers. "If I'd known, I would have sat in the third row for your performance." He met her gaze. "Not that the view could have been better."

Her breath caught, and her bonds fluttered like drifting eiderdown. The heat of his side pressed against hers made her cold and hot at once. He said these things with such ease, such certainty. She fiddled with her curls with her free hand, seeking the comfort of the silky strands. It was terrifying and exhilarating the way he looked at her. The way she felt beneath his stare. She had waited a lifetime for someone to look at her like this. Her bonds stopped their fluttering and tensed. After this night, would anyone ever look at her this way again?

"Guests." The announcer's voice, low and warm, startled Zelandra from her thoughts. Time had passed in a blink, not that she'd dared blink and take Torrick from her sight. The benches had filled while she'd been lost in thought. "Children who wiggle and squirm. The Witch and the Worm."

"Worm?" Torrick blinked, breaking what was left of the spell between them. "I thought you said there was a dragon? What trick is this?"

Zelandra giggled. She'd had much the same reaction when the show joined the circus, wondering what a worm could possibly offer. "Watch."

Torrick narrowed his eyes, but his grin was playful. "All right, but … a worm?"

"Watch." Zelandra used her free hand to turn his head so he faced the ring. She lowered her hand, but he captured her wrist and placed a delicate kiss to her fingers, leaving tingles to storm through her blood. Goddess … she stiffened, waited. The ground did not rumble with the Master's displeasure, and she let herself finish the thought. Goddess, what he did to her. At Grimmfay's end, when he … no. She couldn't think about it. Forcefully, she faced forward, free hand clutching a clump of her hair. She was here with him now, and only now mattered. She would deal with later when it came.

The lights dimmed but for a single spotlight on the narrow rock. So lit, its smooth, rounded surface came into clarity. It was more like a short pole than a rock, but the difference was not important. A low vibrating tone, like wood striking metal, resonated from below. The ring was still, and then a small hole opened in the dirt floor. A worm, maybe the size of Zelandra's index finger, emerged, slithering its small body through and to the base of the pole.

Torrick made a sound between a snort and a huff. "That

is not a dragon."

Zelandra said nothing, waiting. The worm undulated around the base of the pole, it's movements in time to the resonating tone. After it made one full revolution, it stopped, tilted its tiny head to one side, opened its mouth, and started to grow.

A gasp ran through the audience, and Torrick tightened his grip on Zelandra's hand.

Fangs appeared in the worm's mouth. Scales covered its body. A rumble joined the low tone. It was a roar. The worm leaned its head back, horns now protruding from its head, and lunged forward, launching a ball of fire. The gasps turned to screams as the ball stopped a hair's breadth from the edge of the performance ring.

The low tone boomed. The worm recoiled, curling its head toward the back of the ring and revealing the spikes along its back. From a cloud of dense smoke, a person dressed in white with a wand of blackest night—the witch—stepped forth. They raised the wand and waved it back and forth in a pattern to match the low tone. The dragon swayed.

"All right, you win." Torrick leaned close to Zelandra's ear. "That is a dragon."

She grinned at him. "I told you. Now, watch."

The dragon lowered to the ground, coiling its elongated body and slithering back toward the pole. The witch followed, still waving the wand in its hypnotizing pattern. The dragon reached the pole and wriggled up it, wrapping its body around it in a spiral formation. It rested its head atop the pole, and the witch spun into a dance, the dragon's head turning in time with every move. The audience reacted with a mixture of oohs and ahs, and Zelandra had to agree. She'd only seen the show once and given it little thought then, but the control was impeccable. The dragon held such power, and one who seemed weaker ordered it from afar. The dragon did what the witch commanded, a loyal servant.

So, it means being a servant? Torrick's earlier question slammed into Zelandra's heart. She inhaled against its assault, the sound of her breath camouflaged by a well-timed coo from the audience. No, no. It wasn't the same. The dragon was a simple creature with little will of its own. The witch knew better. The dragon was better off relenting to the will of another without question.

We order a task be done, and they do it, no questions asked.

"No." The word came on a whisper. Zelandra fought the connections her mind made, pushing at them with all the might she possessed. But like her bonds compared to the Master's strength, she was no match for the horrible truth finding its way into her bones. She served him. She, Cindell, Bianca, Ori—they all served him. He'd ordered them to find Grenna and Hansten, and they'd jumped to the task without wondering why they should or considering any other options. The children likely had a family, parents who would miss them if they disappeared. Yet, she and her sisters of power thought only of fulfilling what the Master demanded of them. They were servants just like the ones who filled Torrick's palace. Perhaps they held power and command over all other performers, but the Master gave them that power. It was not theirs to own.

In the performance ring, the dragon uncoiled from the pole to join the witch in a leaping, curling fray. The low tones continued to reverberate, shaking Zelandra's insides. She was a dragon. She was might, magic, majesty, but that was all she was. She held no real power, no true control. Everything she did was for the Master and his will. She gripped the strands of her hair and breathed through her nose in a desperate attempt to keep her distress from showing. Torrick was right. How had she not seen? How had this stranger gotten to the heart of her existence when she'd spent countless performances oblivious to it? She was a pawn in the Master's game. A worm to his witch, and like the dragon coiling and darting before her, she had no escape.

The show continued, but Zelandra could no longer see the wonder. All she saw was a worm-turned-dragon dancing and rushing to obey every command made by the witch. How far would the dragon obey? The show only had the creature dance and impress, but if pushed, would it fight? Ensnare? Die? She already did the first two at the Master's command. How far could he push her? What about the other mistresses and everyone else under his rule? The dragon and witch met to either side of the pole. The witch raised their wand, sending orange sparks of flame shooting upward. The dragon threw back its horned head, arching its neck and launching a fireball toward the sky. The orange-yellow flames mingled with the sparks from the witch's wand before spiraling down, down, down toward the witch. With a roar, the dragon launched itself into the air, propelled by some force greater than itself, to meet with the deadly flames just before they engulfed the witch. The creature absorbed the fire, spinning and twisting to capture every last bit of red. Then, it bowed its head and dropped to the ground. The witch pointed their wand, and with a flash of light, the dragon was a worm again. It wriggled in time to the resonating tone—once around the pole and down into the hole from which it had first emerged. The witch drew a circle with their wand. Smoke followed the tracing tip, thickening until it obscured the ring. Little by little, it cleared, leaving all empty and still. The lights faded until the pole was again in spotlight. Then, that light, too, winked away to pitch.

A beat of silence passed, and then the cheers erupted.

"Oh my …" Torrick jumped to his feet with the rest of the room. He sat again, bouncing on the bench like a child. "That was spectacular. Thank you for … Zelandra?" The excitement in his voice vanished, replaced by concern. He took both her hands, uncoiling her fingers from where they gripped her hair, and gazed directly into her eyes. The panic she felt reflected in his pupils after a moment. "Zelandra, what is it? Are you hurt? What's wrong?"

The faintest sense of comfort wedged into her heart, shoving aside just enough of her fear to take root and cocoon her in warmth. Torrick cared. He worried for her. It was more than anyone but Bianca, Cindell, or Ori had ever done, and even their concern paled by comparison. She fought past the realizations threatening to drown her in despair. If Torrick could care this much, there had to be hope. There just had to be.

"I …" Her voice was barely audible over the cheers. She

leaned into him, bringing her lips close to his ear. She could not talk here, not surrounded by the evidence of a world where subservience was praised. She needed quiet and space and somewhere they would not be disturbed. Fortunately, the circus held such a place. "I need to show you something. Will you come with me?"

In response, Torrick stood, bringing her to standing beside him. "Yes."

Hansten

Hansten followed Lady Orianna down a path between tents of milky-yellow and pink. He forced himself to focus on the drab green of her dress. It was the only way to make sure he didn't lose her. The rest of his mind was still back with the harp, watching Grenna leave him over and over again. His heart ached in a way he'd never felt before. Logically, he knew they would grow up, have families of their own, and be apart, but that was different. That was natural. It was how the world worked. What the harp showed him was different. It was Grenna gone from his life. Unreachable. Untraceable. Just … gone. So he focused on Lady Orianna's dress because otherwise his breaths came too fast and his heart pounded. Grimmfay was doing strange things to him, and it was time to go. They'd help find Zelandra because it didn't feel right to leave Lady Orianna so worried, but after that, they were going home.

"Here." Lady Orianna stopped at a juncture where three tents came together—the milky-white, the pink, and a third the dark red of eventide's moon.

Hansten cleared his throat. "Is this where Bianca is?"

Lady Orianna nodded. "Inside." She knocked on the crimson fabric. "Open wide."

The fabric shifted, and suddenly there was a flap where there hadn't been one a moment ago.

Lady Orianna held it open and poked her head through. "Yoo-hoo! Bianca, I seek you."

"Come in," a voice like a high-pitched flute said from inside.

"She is here." Lady Orianna held open the flap and gestured for Hansten and Grenna to go ahead. "Come, to the truth she will steer."

Hansten let Grenna go first before ducking through the opening. Inside, the tent was the same solid dark-red color as the outside, which seemed odd. Many of the tents were very different inside, conforming to whatever show they offered. Maybe this show was simple?

"Oh, you brought … guests."

Hansten jumped. A woman with pale skin, hair darker than the sky, and a billowing crimson gown stood at the other end of the space. She blended into the tent walls so well he hadn't seen her.

"Yes." Lady Orianna entered and let the flap fall closed.

She knocked on the wall, and the opening disappeared. "Your company we bless. And seek Zelandra's ebony dress."

The woman—Lady Bianca—frowned. "Pardon?"

"We're looking for Zelandra." Hansten picked up the explanation. Something about Lady Bianca demanded a directness Lady Orianna's rhymes couldn't give. "She said she'd join us at the harp's show, after she met with you, but she never showed. Is she still here?"

"Zelandra … said she came to see me?" Lady Bianca's frown deepened, and a crease formed between her thin eyebrows. "Zelandra never came to see me. Are you certain that is what she said?"

"Butsy …" Lady Orianna wrung her hands. "That can't be right. If not here, where did she take flight?"

"I don't know," Bianca said, clasping her hands before her. "But I have not seen her since we met to … before the show."

Silence fell, broken only by what sounded like a tiny heartbeat. Hansten's mind raced. He didn't know Zelandra well, but the worry on Lady Orianna's and Lady Bianca's faces told him something was very wrong.

"So," Grenna's small voice broke the quiet, "she's missing?"

"It seems she is," Bianca said.

"A mistress is missing." Lady Orianna swayed and spoke in a sing-song pattern. "Missing, missing, sets my heart twisting. We must discover where she takes cover."

"And soon." Bianca cast a fretful gaze upward. "The grand performance is not far off."

"Grand performance?" Grenna asked.

Lady Bianca smiled tightly. "Soon enough, but first, we need to find Zelandra. A moment." She crossed to a vanity with a heart-shaped mirror and picked up an ivory knife no bigger than her smallest finger. She pricked her thumb, causing a bead of blood to well, and pressed the crimson drop to the glass. Lines of red, blue, and green rushed outward from the mirror's center, starting as a speck and growing into circles.

"Wow!" Grenna darted across to the vanity and gaped. "That's incredible."

Lady Bianca nodded. The ripples continued their pattern—red, blue, green—growing faster, then slower and slower until they stopped, and the mirror showed the reflection of crimson fabric again. A tremor went through Lady Bianca's body. "I … cannot find her."

"Cannot find?" Lady Orianna shifted her weight from one foot to the other. "Cannot find. We are in a bind. Her mind, unkind, caught behind and blind—"

"Ori, stop." Lady Bianca's voice was firm. "Panic will get us nowhere. Zelandra could not have left the circus grounds. She is here somewhere. We will simply have to look for her."

"Look." Lady Orianna whimpered like a lost kitten. "But where to look? Where was she took? How to check every nook?"

"It's okay." Grenna crossed back to Lady Orianna and took one of the young woman's hands between her two small ones. "We'll help. We can split up. That's how they search for people in storybooks, and they always find whoever's lost. If we work together, we'll find her. Right, Hansten?"

Hansten bit his lip before he could object that this wasn't a storybook. Just because people in stories were found didn't mean they'd find Zelandra. He needed to say all those things, but the fear on Lady Orianna's face clawed at his heart, making the words die in his throat. It was the same way Grenna looked when she woke from a nightmare and crawled into his bed, seeking a hug from her big brother. He couldn't leave her. Not like this. He took his place at Grenna's side and grasped Lady Orianna's other hand. "We'll find her. Don't worry."

"Very well." Lady Bianca went to the tent wall through which they'd entered. She knocked, and the opening appeared. "We have no time to lose. Let us go." She stepped through the flap.

"Go." Lady Orianna pulled her hands free and went to the fabric on shaky steps. "We go. We go. To find what we know. To-and-fro." She ducked outside, still sing-song rhyming.

Grenna went next, and Hansten followed, gripping her hand the moment they were outside. "Which way do you think we should go?"

"We?" Grenna halted. "Weren't you listening? We need to split up."

In the back of his head, an alarm bell like the one he'd heard once on a trip into town blared. No. They weren't splitting up. That wasn't what she said inside. The group needed to split up. Lady Orianna and Lady Bianca could search separately while he and Grenna went together. How did Grenna even think he'd let her wander around by herself? "You and I aren't splitting up."

"Why?" Grenna pulled her hand away and straightened,

shoulders square and jaw set. She was a little version of their mother. "Zelandra's missing. We don't have time to argue, and the circus is huge. If we don't all go different ways, we might not find her."

"Grenna." It took all his willpower not to raise his voice. If he shouted or ordered, Grenna would rebel and run off without him. "I understand you're concerned, but Zelandra's a grown woman. She can take care of herself. But if we separate, we might lose each other." The empty feeling of Grenna gone forever from the harp show threatened to choke him. He couldn't lose her. Grimmfay affected her somehow. It pulled her away from him and home, and he couldn't shake the feeling she'd succumb to whatever power the circus held if he wasn't there to stop her. "We're staying together. You can't go off by yourself."

"Yes, I can." She glared. "Zelandra needs us."

"Grenna—"

"No!" Grenna took a big step back. "You think just because you're older you can tell me what to do, treat me like a kid. I'm not a baby anymore. I'm going to look for Zelandra by myself, and you can't stop me." Fast—so fast—she spun and darted toward the opening between the tents.

"Grenna, no!" Hansten lunged, but she slipped from his reach. He stumbled, regained his footing, but by the time he straightened, she was turning a corner and disappearing from sight.

Gone.

His heart skipped a beat, then another. No, no, she couldn't be gone already. His legs found their strength, and he was running past the tents of milky-yellow and pink, out to the main pathway. Grenna had turned right. He turned right and barreled into the stream of circus goers, who suddenly seemed to be converging on his location. There were so many people, and none of them were Grenna. A family of five—two women, one man, and two kids—cut in front of him, forcing him to halt or flatten them. They passed. The world opened in front of him, but there was no Grenna.

No. Where was she? She couldn't have moved so fast. "Grenna!" Hansten wove around laughing guests. They all seemed to step right where he needed to go, and not one looked at the frantic boy in their midst. "Grenna!" She'd only had a few steps head start. She couldn't have gotten far. But something in his gut told him she got farther than would have been possible outside the circus. The ground helped her. The people had split like water around a bolder to let her pass. He didn't know how, but a part of him knew it was true. Grimmfay didn't want him to find his sister. It was ridiculous. Grimmfay was a circus. It didn't have a mind of its own.

Or it shouldn't have, but it did. He felt it opposing him. No, not opposing him. Just opposing his desire to find Grenna and leave. Whispers circled his ears. They urged him to give up, give in, stay. Grenna wanted to stay. Didn't he want to stay? He'd seen amazing things. Fantastic things.

"No!" He slammed his hands over his ears, but it didn't block the whispers. It didn't block the little voice inside him he'd been trying to silence since before they arrived. The one that told him the circus was where he belonged. The one that wanted to live in a place of magic and wonder. The one that, even now, saw a glowing ball of silver hovering across the path and drew him like a moth to the candles his family sat around on warm summer nights.

He wanted it. He wanted it all. He wanted it like nothing he'd ever wanted before. It would be so easy to take what Grimmfay offered. To be part of the magic, the majesty. He'd be the boy of the woods. Trees and animals would bend to his will. Squirrels would chatter in his ear, and birds would sing to him and him alone. He and Grenna would be so happy …

Grenna!

"No!" He staggered away from the flickering silver light. No. He didn't belong here. Grenna didn't belong here. The circus's syrupy tendrils wrapped around his mind, lulling him into its snare. He fought it. Fought it harder than he'd seen animals with their legs caught in traps fight. For whatever reason, the circus wanted them.

But it wouldn't get them.

He curled his hands into fists. The flow of people passed by. He found an opening and joined the stream to wherever it went. His heart beat steady now, and he focused straight ahead. Not at the colorful tents, the open performance rings. Not at the ebony sky, azure stars, crimson moon, or sparkling jade grass. The circus would not claim him. He would find Grenna and get them out of here no matter what it took.

Zelandra

Zelandra wove through the crowd in a haze. Her body felt so cold everywhere except where Torrick gripped her hand. There, warmth enveloped her flesh and bone, somehow giving the rest of her enough energy to put one foot in front of the other. Everything felt muted. The brightest blues and greens fell flat. Grimmfay's lilting music could have been any tune at any place. Even her sky, in all its magnificent expanse and shining glory, couldn't reach her beneath the layer of ice cutting her off from the world.

"Where are we going?" Torrick asked close to her ear. He sounded concerned and confused, both rightly so.

"Not yet." It was all she'd said since they'd left the worm

performance. She had her reasons, and she would share them soon enough when it felt safe. Until then, all her concentration went to moving forward through the crowd.

Finally, the path opened into a circular area. More paths led off to the left and right. Ahead, a tent of deep green waited, swaying gently in a nonexistent breeze. Zelandra crossed to it on quickening strides. The quiet within called her, offering its silent strength. When she was almost there, a flap appeared in the fabric. She reached for it, fingers seeking and finding the comfort of smooth tree bark. Her bonds settled. "After you." She opened the flap and followed Torrick through, stopping just inside to avoid colliding with him. She sidestepped, let the flap fall, and faced the Enchanted Forest.

"It's … a forest … in a tent." Torrick's voice held the same wonder it had when they'd met in the maze of mirrors.

"It's the Enchanted Forest, the safest place in Grimmfay." She bit her lip. It was true. Disloyal, but true. For no reason she, Bianca, Cindell, or Ori could determine, the Master had less of a presence here. They hadn't met beneath the trees to talk away from his awareness much, but when they had, those moments were full of embraces, tears, laughter, and the kinds of secrets only shared in hushed whispers.

"I don't …" Torrick shook his head. "How is this possible?"

"The circus is full of wonders." It was both an answer and no answer at all. She tugged him forward onto a gray rock speckled with ebony, azure, crimson, and jade flecks. "Come."

She walked ahead along a path that had not been there

before. Such was the way of the wood, Cindell had once told them. A cool breeze captured the loose tendrils of hair around Zelandra's face, making them dance to the tune of chittering squirrels and chirping birds. The wood made its own paths and kept its own company. It was both part of the circus and its own place, and it offered no explanation nor made any apologies. It simply was, and its simplicity cradled Zelandra's heart in comfort. Trees glowing the faintest silvery green passed in her periphery. She inhaled, steady, finding Grimmfay's sweetness replaced by something earthy and ancient. It gave her the courage to speak of the emotions the worm's performance stirred, but it was not time, not yet. The path laid itself, and it had to be followed.

At last, the path ended at a pool of water surrounded by stones the pure blue of a robin's egg. Zelandra stopped on the second-to-last stone, unable or unwilling to go farther. Which, she did not know.

"Here?" Torrick squeezed her hand. His voice was so gentle, so understanding. It was unlike any voice that had ever, ever spoken to her.

Its gentleness let her release a slow breath and finally speak. "Here." She gestured to the pool, still and dark as a starless sky. It did not reflect the trees above and never would. "This water shows you what you most need to see, but only if you are the first to look. I … need to see if the things I feel are true, but …" Her voice trailed into a ragged whisper.

"I'm here." Torrick released her hand and wrapped his arm around her shoulders, pulling her close. His free hand came up to cup her cheek. "Whatever it is, whatever you see, we'll face it together."

The comfort in his tone and the firmness in his embrace melted her trembling away. Was this what true support felt like? It seemed she could do anything, conquer any obstacle, so long as Torrick stood by her side. His calm reassurance flowed into her everywhere they touched, filling her with the resolve she needed. At the beginning of this eventide, she never would have thought to visit the pool. Now, she needed to.

"Thank you." She leaned into him, gathering any last reserves of strength, before extracting herself from his embrace, stepping upon the final stone in the path, and perching on the blue stones surrounding the water. Torrick's presence filled the space between them, offering everything she needed and more. With another fortifying breath, she leaned forward and peered into the pool.

A daytime sky—so much bluer than Cindell's blue—shone down on a forest of green trees like and nothing like the ones in the Enchanted Forest. The view roamed through the woods, passing trunks and shrubs along its journey. A family of squirrels scurried by, and she could almost hear the pitter of their tiny feet upon the forest floor. Onward and onward, twists and turns, until the trees opened to a clearing.

A familiar clearing.

Sunlight dappled the greenery. The ghost of smells long suppressed tickled her nose, and she knew before the view turned to reveal the tower of ivory stone that the pool had brought her … there.

"Zelandra!" That voice. It called with such carefree joy, such motherly love. Such lies. "Let down your hair for me."

A beat, and then Zelandra's golden curls cascaded from high above to dangle with their ends barely touching the ground. The view rose up and up and up until it reached a window. The view moved through but then blurred and shifted to a nighttime scene, distinguishable only by the lit candles around a room she knew better than the trappings of her own mind. Three figures stood in the space—one with power, one that cowered, one a shield. The muffled tones of raised voices flitted about her ears, and then the figure with power was moving, pushing, and the cowering one was out the window. The shield lunged after the tumbling form but was grabbed and yanked away.

Another blur. Darkness. Sorrow. Tears on two sets of cheeks, one with shorn locks dangling barely to shaking shoulders. Whispered promises halted the sobs, offered power. Power for her, to change fate, to escape, to see punishment where it was deserved. Power that gave her strength to do what the promiser requested and nothing more. Promises that moved her from one life of servitude to another and tricked her with its feeling of strength. Terrible things were done. Strength was restored. Confidence followed.

It was all a lie. All orchestrated by him for his benefit, not hers. Not any of theirs. He was the witch. She was the worm. What had she done?

The final image faded, leaving the pool a circle of darkness once more. Zelandra stared into its unbroken surface, her hands tightly woven together in her lap. Her breaths came in ragged sighs. Torrick was right. She was a servant. Her power was nothing more than a well-crafted illusion. The Master gave it to her so she could break free of the bonds holding her, only to then do his bidding. Eventide after eventide, she performed, amazed, dangled the circus like a treat the way her hair had dangled from that tower. This night, she would have ripped two innocent children from their lives and family simply because the Master willed it. What kind of monster was he? What kind of monster was she?

A choked sound escaped her. Not this kind.

"Zel?" Torrick's voice bordered on panic.

"It was all a lie." She forced her fingers free of their grips, uncoiled her hands, and stood to face him. Her breaths felt too fast, too little. "He gave me power, but it wasn't for me. It was for him." She swallowed around the lump threatening to cut off her air. "You were right. I'm nothing more than a servant." Saying the words made them too real. She crumpled, gathering herself into a ball on the stone of the path.

"Zel." Torrick was there, holding her, his warmth battling her cold. He cradled her against him, wiping tears away with a gentle stroke of his thumb. "It's all right. You know now. Knowing is half the battle. There must be a way. We can find it together."

There was no way. The Master himself had said so. Grimmfay took what it wished and never let it go.

But had he not also said the power was for her?

She blinked. Had he lied? He said he could not lie, and that had always felt realer than anything else. But he could bend the truth. The power was for her, literally—it ran through her veins.

If she took apart what else she knew, perhaps there was a grain of something she could use to win true freedom.

"Zel?"

"There might be a way." There had to be. She would not stay here now that she knew the truth—the circus was nothing more than a grander tower. "At the end of each performance, the circus pulls everything of its own to itself, but it cannot extend beyond the outer wall. At least, I don't think it can."

Torrick's eyes glinted with a spark of hope. "So, what are you saying?"

If only she knew. The memory was halfway invisible, but she still saw it—a family of four, two parents and two children, stragglers after the grand performance. One of the children didn't want to leave, stood within the gate crying. Something in the sky had shifted, and the ground had somehow responded, moving the child over the threshold, back to the world outside Grimmfay. He was not part of the circus, and the circus could not take him.

"I don't know if it will work." She inhaled, exhaled, faced him with a grim determination she had never felt before. "I don't even know if it makes sense, but Grimmfay can only take what belongs to it and what is within its bounds. If part of me were … outside the walls when it closed. Maybe …"

"Maybe it couldn't take you."

She nodded. "I'm basing this on something half-remembered and foggy."

Torrick grinned. "Sometimes, those are the best things on which to form a theory." His grin vanished. "So, part of you leaves the circus. How? It's not as if I can cut—"

Zelandra raised one hand, calling to where the bonds rattled in her chest. A delicate ebony-colored chain grew from her palm. It jangled softly, wrapping around her wrist. With a slicing thought, she broke it from the source. Pain, sudden and sharp, struck her heart and then was gone. She held up the chain. "My power." She used her other hand to open one of Torrick's and then carefully laid the chain in his palm. "The moment the grand performance ends, take this off Grimmfay's grounds. Maybe if it is no longer within the circus, Grimmfay won't recognize me as part of it anymore."

"Why wait?" He closed his fingers around the chain. "I should take it now."

"No." She shook her head. "I don't want to take the chance of the Master sensing it somehow. The less time he has to react, the better. I don't … I can't … if he …" She gripped her skirts. This was madness, stupidity. The Master knew all. He would know this, haul her back, imprison her. She would be a servant for the rest of her existence.

"Zel." Torrick wrapped her tighter in his arms. "It will be all right."

"But what if it's not?" Tremors shook her, and try as she might, she couldn't stop them. "What if I can't escape. What if I never see the sun again? I can't live this life, knowing you're out there."

"You won't have to." He cupped her cheek again and met her gaze. "Listen to me now. If it doesn't work, if for some reason you are pulled back in, I will come for you. I'll find Grimmfay and tear it down tent by tent if I have to. He won't keep you. I won't let him."

The strength in his voice pooled like liquid warmth low in her belly. She'd thought she was so strong—escaping her old life, wielding bonds with the precision of a hardened warrior. But here in Torrick's arms, all that supposed strength reformed into something new and incredible and terrifying. It melded with his own power to create something unique and commanding. It drew her to him, and she felt it draw him to her.

"I want you." She breathed the words on a puff of air.

Fire blazed in Torrick's eyes. He leaned forward. She moved to meet him, and then her lips were against his. Her bonds and heart stirred with desire. The kiss was everything she'd ever dreamed one could be. Gentle and forceful. Soft and demanding. He tasted of the woods and metal. His lips were the smoothest silk. She opened to him, felt him open to her until she no longer knew where he began and she ended. This was what she'd waited her entire life for. This was every dream she'd never had and never knew she wanted. He was the culmination of all she yearned for, and she tied herself to him with every bond she had.

Sometime later, Zelandra came back to herself through the sound of Torrick's heartbeat. She rested her head on his chest, and he held her as if she were the most precious piece of porcelain. She gripped the moment tight, wrapping it in layers of chain and rope and tucking it beside her heart. If this plan failed, this moment would have to sustain her for a lifetime of lifetimes.

"I love you." Torrick spoke low, his lips brushing her ear.

Zelandra's blood hummed. Tingles raced through her, warm then cool then warm. They flitted around the hum, beside it but never touching it.

Because the hum wasn't from Torrick. It was Grimmfay calling her back for the grand performance. It was almost time. Amazing how she hadn't recognized it. In every past performance, the tone was clear and bright and couldn't have possibly been mistaken for anything else. Further proof she belonged with Torrick, not within the Master's control. He couldn't call her, couldn't keep her.

At least, not after this night.

"I love you, too." She pressed her lips to his, quick, fleeting even. "The grand performance approaches, and I must prepare."

His embrace tightened. "I look forward to seeing your final performance."

Despite everything, she smiled. She wanted to amaze him with bonds just one more time. This performance would mean more to her than any other because it would be for him. "I look forward to after."

He returned her fleeting kiss, and then his arms were loosening, releasing her. She sat and got to standing, the forest feeling so far from her now.

"Umm." Torrick glanced around and then quirked one eyebrow at her. "So … how do we get out of here?"

Zelandra blinked then giggled. Right. He didn't know. "The wood makes a way where one is needed." She traced the outline of a door in the air and twisted its invisible handle. The air parted, revealing a path different from the one where they'd entered the forest's tent.

Torrick's jaw went slack. "How …?"

"The wood makes its own rules." Zelandra motioned for him to go through.

He did, and she followed back into the sights and sounds of the circus. After the silence, Grimmfay's lilting song invaded her ears. The sweet aroma on the breeze no longer smelled of things wanted. Now, it sickened and suffocated her. The grand performance couldn't come fast enough.

"Where do you need to go from here?" Torrick asked.

Zelandra shook away the music and scent. Technically, she hadn't needed to return to the main circus. She could have summoned bonds to bring her back to her chamber from the forest. She'd wanted just another moment with him, a feeling that hadn't lessened with gaining that moment. "Anywhere. The circus makes paths for us." But she didn't move. An invisible force kept her rooted beside him. She had to get away. So long as she could see him, she wouldn't have the strength to leave. "I'll take my leave from there." She pointed to a path between tents of orange-yellow and light purple. And then didn't move. She had to do this. "I'll see you later."

"Yes."

Go. The silent reprimand got her to lift her foot, and from there, her body got the message. She turned away, took heavy step after heavy step until she reached the tents. Her heart begged for one more glance. What if this was the last time he'd be so close? She didn't dare turn. If she did, she'd run back to him. She'd be late for the grand performance. The magic would retrieve her, alerting the Master and destroying her one chance. It wasn't worth a final glimpse of Torrick's face. She continued down the path, eyes fixed straight ahead, ears tuning out the music, nose, not smelling.

"Zelandra?" That voice. It was familiar. And young. And …

Hansten stood ahead on the path, shoulders squared and hands in fists at his sides. He stalked toward her and stopped in front of her, forcing her to halt. "What happened to you? Why did you lie to us? You never met with Mistress Bianca, and now Grenna's gone, and it's all your fault."

Hansten

Zelandra staggered back a step, and the color drained from her face. "What?" Her voice was a hoarse whisper.

Hansten's indignant anger snuffed out like the flame of a candle. He'd been wandering the circus for ... he didn't know how long exactly, but he'd been sure that, if he found Zelandra, she would have an explanation, excuses, and apologies. He had not at all expected her to be taken aback by Grenna's disappearance.

Zelandra recovered, shaking her head and sending her golden curls tumbling. "I ... we need to talk, but not here." She took Hansten's hand, and ebony ropes twined with their fingers, tying him to her.

"What—" Hansten's question was cut off as the circus

went dark. What was she doing? Was she taking him captive? Goddess, no. He'd made a mistake, a terrible mistake. He yanked his hand back, but the ropes, soft as the silk shirt his father once bought for a wedding, didn't give at all.

Then, light in the darkness. The ropes were gone. Hansten went absolutely still, blinking against the feeble brightness. He was in a room of darkness, but somehow, the darkness also glowed a little. Where had she taken him?

"I'm sorry if I startled you." Zelandra released his hand and gripped her hair, running her fingers through the strands over and over like a small child seeking comfort. "This room is within the private part of the circus but doesn't contain enough light for a reflection. It should be safe."

Reflection? Safe? "What are you talking about? What's going on? Where are we? How—"

"A moment, and I will explain."

Hansten snapped his mouth shut. The room was dim but not dim enough to hide how distraught Zelandra was. The rasp in her voice made her sound hundreds of years old. Hansten drew in a deep breath. Realistically, he could wait for her to collect her emotions. He didn't have Grenna and wouldn't leave without her. The circus's grand performance—whatever it was—was still to come, which meant Grimmfay wouldn't close its gates yet, and he needed Zelandra's help.

Zelandra mimicked his deep breath. She exhaled, released her hair, straightened, and clasped her hands before her. "I need to tell you something, but you must wait and listen to the whole story. Please."

Hansten's gut twisted. By her tone, this news was not going to be something he wanted to hear, but that didn't change any of the conclusions he'd just come to. "All right."

Zelandra nodded, closed her eyes, and opened them. "The Master tasked me and the other mistresses with bringing you into Grimmfay's hold."

"You … what?" Hansten stiffened, tensing to run, hide, do whatever he had to do to escape this place she'd brought him to. "I—"

"Please, hear me out." Her voice was pleading, and she hurried on before he could interrupt. "He tasked us with this, and I initially intended to comply." She swallowed. "But … something has changed me since the beginning of eventide. I've realized I am a prisoner within the circus's walls and have seen the freedom beyond its gates." A soft smile curved her lips, making her even more beautiful, even with tension forming lines in her face. The smile faded, and she met Hansten's gaze, her own calm and steady. "I am sorry for my deception. I know nothing can make up for what I almost did, but I want to help you and your sister get away before it's too late."

The words sent a shiver down Hansten's spine. He didn't fully understand everything about the circus, but Zelandra's confession confirmed so many things he suspected. Grimmfay had been affecting him. The call and lure he'd felt since before he came—still felt with an intensity that made him want to scream—was real. It wanted him. It pulled at him. It wanted and pulled at Grenna with the same strength, but unlike him, she'd listened, and she was gone now, maybe beyond his reach.

No. He couldn't think that way. Zelandra just said she wanted to help them both get away, not only him. There was still hope. Grenna could be saved. He still didn't know if he fully trusted Zelandra, but he didn't have much of a choice. If he wandered alone, he may just as easily stumble further into Grimmfay's snare. Zelandra understood how the circus worked and how to fight it. He needed her.

"Why?" The question slipped past Hansten's lips without him knowing exactly what he was asking about. "Why does Grimmfay want Grenna and me?"

She shook her head. "I am not privy to the Master's whims. He shows us what he wishes, and we secure it for him. There is no room for failure, no place for excuses if his desires are not met. This night, I've learned I am worth more than his anger. If I can escape, I will, and I will do everything in my power to make sure he doesn't keep you or your sister." Her green eyes sparkled. "My parting act of defiance."

Hansten stared at her. She was an adult, and she'd learned so much in one night. Maybe growing older and becoming a man didn't mean he would know everything. Maybe he'd continue learning and growing for the rest of his life. Two days ago, that idea would have terrified him. He had no respect for Grimmfay anymore, but if the circus offered him this lesson to carry forward, he'd take it.

"Thank you." It felt insufficient, but he didn't know what

else to say. "So, what do we do now?"

Zelandra held up one hand. A length of chain grew from her open palm, curling around her wrist with a tiny jingling sound. Her forehead creased, and the chain snapped free, tumbling until she caught it with one swift motion. "Your sister will attend the grand performance. She will be pulled to it. I have set events in motion, and if I have any chance of escape, it will happen the moment the performance is over. Find Grenna, and make sure both of you are holding on to this chain when the show ends. If my plan works, it will bring you beyond Grimmfay's grounds." She held out the chain.

Hansten took it. The metal was smooth and the links delicate, but something told him it was the strongest chain he'd ever seen or ever would see. He let its cool weight settle in his palm like the hope coiling in his belly. "And what if it doesn't work?" He hated to ask but had to know.

Zelandra knelt so she was at his level and took his shoulders, her grasp gentle but firm. "If it doesn't work, run. Run as fast as you can for the gates and don't look back. Don't let Grenna look back. She'll want to. I can't tell you how much she'll want to, but she mustn't, not even once you are outside Grimmfay's grounds. Run until the sun has risen. Only then will you be safe."

"But what about you? If it doesn't work, can I help you?"

"Never mind me. You must run."

"But—"

"Run." She released his shoulder to curl one hand around his chin, forcing him to make eye contact. "Promise you won't come back for me. Promise me, if the chain fails, you will take your sister and get away from here." Her eyes darkened, and she set her jaw. "If it fails, I will fight. You cannot be here when I do. Promise."

Her voice dipped low on the last words, and Hansten shivered. What he'd seen in The Heights and this chain she'd created—they were nothing compared to the power she held. "All right, I promise."

"Good." She released him and straightened. "Now, I must prepare, and you must go before anyone finds you here." She moved to one dark wall and rapped three times, the sound muffled. A beat of stillness passed, and then a doorway appeared, showing the circus beyond. Just like in Lady Bianca's tent.

Hansten shivered again—he couldn't ever remember shivering so much outside of winter. With halting steps, he crossed to the doorway and passed through. The moment he was back among the crowds, the doorway vanished, leaving him engulfed by Grimmfay's sickly saccharine smell and lulling song. Stay. Enjoy. Be. The messages bombarded his nose and ears. Grimmfay wanted him, offered him everything, everything. His own performance, a lifetime of fun for him and Grenna. He saw it in his mind. They laughed. They never cried again. Throngs of children and adults alike were mesmerized by them. He was happy, so happy. It was his. It was all his. His heart floated with lightness. Yes. Yes! The circus promised …

Promised.

Zelandra.

"No." Hansten gasped and shoved the images away. He

slammed back to himself, panting, unable to draw enough air untainted by this place. People bustled past, chattering and laughing and sparing no glances for the struggling boy in their midst. Easy, it would be so easy to give in, to take everything Grimmfay gave and more. He couldn't. Maybe it would mean joy for the rest of his life, but it wouldn't be real. It would be whatever the circus and its master told it to be. He wouldn't give in, and he wouldn't let Grenna be lost. He had to find this grand performance and his sister.

He drew in another breath of tainted air and stepped into the crowd, getting caught in its flow. Everyone seemed to be moving with purpose in the same direction. He let the current carry him around colorful tents blurred by his movement, down a path and toward a towering big top he hadn't seen before.

Because it hadn't been there. Again, he didn't know how he knew. This had to be where the grand performance would take place. The crowd forced him closer, and the shifting lights above the structure became clear. A high-heeled shoe the color of Grimmfay's stars spun in a slow circle. Then in a blink, it was gone, replaced by a spinning wheel the color of Lady Orianna's gown. Was the spindle related to her somehow? Before Hansten could think too much about it, the shape darkened into a tower the shade of the sky and Zelandra's gown.

Hansten's body urged him to stop, but the relentless river of the crowd kept him moving. The tower was a symbol of what kept Zelandra within the circus. More things he just knew. Which meant the spinning wheel meant something to Lady Orianna and the shoe was relevant to someone. Another mistress? A dark-red apple with a single bite replaced Zelandra's tower—the red of Lady Bianca's dress and the pale inner fruit white like her flesh—and then the crowd herded Hansten through an opening in the big top's side, taking the changing objects from view.

Inside, rows and rows of benches ringed a central performance area. The chattering crowd swept him toward the front of the nearest section, and Hansten elbowed his way out of the flow, not apologizing to the man he knocked in the stomach. Not that the man would have heard him. Judging by the enraptured grin on his face, he hadn't even felt the jab. More and more people passed, and Hansten studied them from an empty space between two rows. Tall people, short people. Adults and children with blonde and brown and gray and orange hair, even. But none was Grenna. Where was his sister? The bench in front of him started to fill. Hansten scrambled over the benches toward the back of the room. He needed a wall to stand against so he could see the entire space. It was the only hope he had of finding his sister among so many people. When he reached the final bench, he stood on it, putting his head above most of the adults who passed by, oblivious to his presence. He started at one end of the room and turned his head ever-so-slowly, searching every face, every tuft of hair for Grenna's smile or familiar brown locks. Zelandra said Grenna would be here—she wouldn't be able to resist. Benches filled around the room. Row after row of elated circus-goers met Hansten's search, none of them his sister. Where was she? Could Zelandra have been wrong? What if she was lost or hurt and couldn't—

There.

She was two sections over at the end of a row toward the middle. She bounced in her seat, gaze fixed on the performance ring as if it held all the wonder in the world.

Hansten's heart sank. The circus had its talons around her heart, like the dragon clutching gold nuggets in a storybook their father brought from one of his many trips into town. His sister's heart was precious to Grimmfay somehow, but he would not let it keep her. He hopped off the bench and worked his way around the room to the row of benches where Grenna sat. He was getting her back, no matter what.

Zelandra

Zelandra watched Hansten until the door completely closed. The moment the last of Grimmfay disappeared, she sagged, curling her hair around her in an inadequate embrace. With a whisp of thought, ropes coiled from her palms, up her arms, and around her shoulders. Their softness caressed her skin with uncomfortable relief. The bonds were her life. They were what gave her a second chance, allowed her to escape one gilded cage for another. What if Torrick was yet another beautiful prison? What if she came to regret the choice to follow him? She barely knew him, but at the same time, it was as if she'd known him forever and had just been waiting for him to find her.

"Goddess." The invocation wasn't even a whisper. The ground

had trembled for much less, but it didn't move at all. Perhaps the Master was distracted, or perhaps his attention was required elsewhere. Whatever the case, she was grateful he'd missed her transgression. His wrath over such small things made her shiver. Torrick offered her a path away from such belittling fears. Even if a life with him turned out to be another cage, she would at least be out in the world, free to choose again. She'd chosen Grimmfay, after all.

Another low tone echoed through her blood—the last call. The grand performance awaited, and she could dawdle no longer. She shook her shoulders so her hair once again fell behind them. The ropes around her arms dissolved into nothingness. Their disappearance lifted a weight from her flesh and heart. She could do this. She would perform and fight for her freedom. She deserved this chance. Another thought sent her into the shadows and to her chamber. The ebony fabric draping the walls, once calming, now suffocated the space. Her vanity table with its oval mirror stood like a bastion against one wall. From its table, crimson and azure seemed to glow against the black surface.

A flurry of knocks came at the door. "Zelandra."

Cindell. Zelandra's bonds rattled with restless uncertainty. What was she doing here so close to the grand performance? A fleeting glance to the mirror confirmed she held the expression of a cornered animal. A single deep breath was all she got. "Yes." Her voice tremored, hopefully too little for anyone else to notice.

The door opened. Cindell stepped through, followed by Bianca. No Ori. Zelandra's heart skipped a beat, causing her bonds to jerk still and then quiver uncontrollably. She blinked, both to convey confusion and to give herself a moment. "What are you doing here? The grand performance starts soon. Where's Ori?"

"In her room." Cindell clasped her hands before her. She lifted her head and fixed suspicious brown eyes on Zelandra. "As to the performance, we know. The question is, do you?"

"Orianna and the children came to find me." Bianca closed the door with a soft click. The concern in her birdlike voice brought its pitch lower than normal. "You told her you had a meeting with me, but we discussed no such meeting. Why did you lie to them?"

Zelandra's heart sped. Her bonds shuddered. The entire thing felt like a quake in her chest—beat, shudder, shudder, thump. They caught her in a lie. The worst lie. She had no explanation, nothing to ease Cindell's suspicion or Bianca's questions. She opened her mouth to say something, anything.

"I'm sorry." It was as good a start as any. "I … meant to find you, Bianca, but I got sidetracked." The lies tumbled off her tongue, tasting bitter and sweet. Lying to Cindell and Bianca made her ache to her toes. They'd been there for her through so much. They'd held her while she cried, celebrated outstanding performances with her, even once kept her chains from tearing apart the piper's door while she raged against the injustice of guests who dragged their children from the circus for daring to want a treat. They were more than sisters, and here she stood, lying because of a man who'd offered a sky beyond the one she already had.

"Is that all?" Bianca curled her fingers around the pulsing jewel at her throat. "You can tell us. We're just worried about you."

Cindell grunted. Bianca was worried. Cindell might be, too, but she also didn't believe the lies, not fully. She was the one to convince.

"Yes." Zelandra forced her voice not to shake. "I got distracted for longer than I meant to. I didn't intend to worry you."

A final tone reverberated through Zelandra's blood. She saw the moment Cindell and Bianca heard it too. Cindell straightened, and Bianca flinched. The grand performance began with Bianca in a glass box like a coffin, and the experience matched too closely the haunting one from her past.

"It is time." Cindell spread her hands, palms down. "We will continue this discussion after the performance." Twin spears of glass grew from her palms until they met the carpet with muffled thunks. Cindell brought them together before her in a crash of shattering shards. They ballooned into a cloud of azure, and when it cleared, she was gone.

"Always the dramatic one." Bianca shook her head. "Perform well, Zelandra." She tilted her head, and blood gathered at the base of her skirt. Up and up and up it funneled, draping her in a curtain and taking her away.

"You too." Zelandra brought one hand to her lips. The displays of power would normally have filled her with pride. Tonight, they only showed her how little true control Cindell and Bianca held over their lives. They did amazing things but only to go to the next performance required by the Master. She could not hold it against them or hate them for it any more than she could begrudge the bonds that had finally calmed enough for her to draw a deep breath. They'd all made their choices, and her new feelings told her there was more to escape than a handsome prince. She wanted to feel the sun on her face, wanted to have power of her own that didn't extend only to making someone else happy.

"I'm sorry." Tears gathered in her eyes. She blinked them back. Leaving Cindell, Bianca, and Ori hurt like clawing her skin with her fingernails. It would hurt them just as much, but she had to do it. If all went according to plan, there would be no continued discussion, no goodbyes or apologies or explanations. They'd been her everything, but they were not everything. If one of them had the same chance, she would want them to take it. The justification kept her together as she called up her bonds, enfolded herself in their shadows, and went to what would, with any luck, be her last performance.

Grenna

"Guests." A voice, low and serious, spoke at the far left of the tent. Any last sound from the audience faded to nothing.

Grenna stilled. She didn't dare move. She barely dared to breathe. This was it. This was the grand performance. Rightness filled her heart. This was what everything had been pulling her toward since she arrived at the circus. No, her whole life had led to this moment. Something life-changing would happen during this show. She just knew it!

"Children of all ages. This eventide, you have seen wonders beyond your wildest whims." The voice moved across the tent, ending its sentence directly behind where Grenna sat. Its tone curled around her like the warmest hug, and she settled back into its waiting arms.

“You have witnessed feats like you have never thought possible.” The voice moved to Grenna’s right, leaving her shivering in the absence of its embrace. “You have observed things your senses tell you must not be real—” the voice swooped in an upward arc— “but that your heart says are more real than reality itself.” It delivered the words in a circle from above.

Grenna tilted her head up. Her breaths came shallow, and her heart seemed to reach for the voice.

“All you have seen.” The voice traveled in smaller and smaller circles. “All you have witnessed and observed have been but a trick of the light.”

Light flashed to her left. To her right, the shape of a high-heeled shoe formed and then was gone.

“It has been a deception of shadow.”

Directly above, the darkness grew darker somehow. The outline of a tower formed in the air, and Grenna gasped. It was the tower from Zelandra’s performance. She blinked, and the tower disappeared, returning the darkness to its lighter pitch.

“It has been a memory of something never known.” Across the performance ring, the outline of an apple hovered in mid-air and then vanished.

“An echo of what could be.”

Somewhere, a wolf howled. The sound lifted the hairs at the back of Grenna’s neck, but she didn’t shrink back or curl into a ball like when wolves howled outside her house at night. This wolf was harmless. She knew it in the same way she knew so many other things about the circus—deep in her unquestioning heart. Far to her right, a spinning wheel appeared, rotated once, and then was gone. The wolf howl faded, and the yips of foxes replaced it. Crows cawed. Bluebirds whistled in tune with the squeaks of mice. Pigs squealed. Tiny wings and feet fluttered and pattered to a thunderous roar. The sound pressed down around Grenna, and she pressed her hands to her ears. Still, they grew louder, louder, like nothing the woods had ever sounded like.

And then, with a final explosive shout, they silenced.

The quiet jolted through her like lightning. Slowly, she uncovered her ears, waiting for the noise to come back. When it didn't, she lowered her hands and strained to hear any sound in the new silence.

"Grenna."

Her heart skipped a beat. Her name. Was her name part of the performance? Did they choose a guest to be part of the show? Her heart's beats became desperate. Please, please, let it be her.

"Grenna." A hand settled on her arm.

Her silent hopes shattered into broken pieces and scratched at her insides. It wasn't the show. The circus wasn't asking her to be part of it. It was Hansten. He sat beside her—somehow, there was room on the bench where there hadn't been before—and kept his hand firmly on her elbow.

"Grenna, thank the Goddess I found you." Hansten's voice was low and fierce. "Listen, after this performance, we have to—"

"Lady Orianna, Mistress of Thorns." The voice overtook Grenna's ears, pulling her whole being back to Grimmfay and the amazement she knew was waiting. Above the left side of the performance ring, a single thorn, like the ones on the shrubs behind her cottage, appeared.

"I found Zelandra and—"

"Lady Cindell, Mistress of Glass." Again, the voice cut her brother off. This time, a single shard of glass formed above the right of the ring.

"She said we—"

"Lady Bianca, Mistress of Blood." A drop of blood hovered above the far side of the ring.

"Have to—"

"Lady Zelandra, Mistress of Bonds." A dark link of chain emerged from the shadows above Grenna's head.

"The might, the magic, the majesty."

"Touch the chain and—"

"Hansten, shush." Grenna whirled on him, glaring. "The performance is starting. You're being rude."

The objects above flashed brightly before disappearing. In the light, Grenna saw the hurt and fear on Hansten's face. A tiny part of her heart felt for him before the rest of it reminded her he wanted to take her away from the circus and back to a life she didn't want. She pulled her arm from his grip and faced forward. She wouldn't go. Not without a fight.

"Grimmfay." The voice spoke from above the center of the ring. It's sound faded little by little and drifted down, joining a low beating sound like a drum. No, a heart? The rhythm traveled across the ring, getting faster and louder.

Suddenly, red light shone from above. It lit a box at the performance ring's center that hadn't been there a moment ago. Someone lay in the box, and Grenna strained, leaning forward to see. The drumming heartbeat grew faster, faster, and the light grew brighter, revealing the figure in the box was Lady Bianca. She laid perfectly still even as the drums crashed like thunder. A boom greater than the others shook the air. The box shattered, shards flying in every direction. People screamed or flinched back. Grenna didn't move. The shards wouldn't hurt her.

In the ring, Lady Bianca shifted to standing and opened one hand, palm up. A heart of blood formed in the air. She lowered her hand, somehow bringing the heart to hover before her chest. The blood cascaded down so her billowing skirt sparkled in the dim light. At the floor, the blood pooled and spread, racing toward the edge of the ring.

More screams filled the air, all cut short by a cracking sound. From the base of the ring's outer edge, walls of glass, thorn, and shadow grew and linked, stopping the blood in its tracks. Lights flashed around the tent. Far to the right, Ori stood tall in a queen-like gown of jade. Her honey-blonde hair whipped and snapped around her face, and a crown of thorns perched atop her head. Grenna's breath left in a rush. Ori was too simple a name for the jade mistress. She was Orianna—Lady Orianna—as she glided toward the ring on confident, steady strides. She was so beautiful, so powerful. She was everything Grenna wanted to be. From the other end of the ring, blue tried to steal Grenna's attention, and somewhere in the background, Zelandra's golden hair caught her eye for a moment, but none of it could steal her admiration from Orianna. Hansten's presence was still solid beside her on the bench, but he may as well have been back at their cottage. She was physically close to him, but emotionally, she was far away and gone. Grimmfay was her future, not collecting berries and learning to keep house. Lady Orianna crossed the barrier into the performance ring and raised her delicate hands. Vines lashed from her fingertips, their cracking sounds mixing with tinkling glass chimes and the whoosh of blood and rope rushing to clash at a central point. Green, red, blue, and black tangled in a battle. The crowd reacted. Babies cried. A few grunts and gasps punctuated the air.

Grenna savored it all like the lebkuchen her mother made on special occasions. The bread was sweet and warm and filling—nothing like the fight in the ring. But the making of the bread was magic, just like what Lady Orianna and the others did. Just like what Grenna wanted to do. If she'd wondered before, she was sure now. She was staying with the circus. It would take more than Hansten's fear to take her from the life Grimmfay offered. If she had to fight like Lady Orianna fought right now to stay, she would.

Zelandra

Thrill and disgust mixed in Zelandra's blood. Around her, chains and ropes tangled in a deadly dance with glass and blood and thorn. It wasn't truly deadly—the Master would never allow such a thing—but for the first time, she saw the frightening clarity of the grand performance. It was meant to amaze, to awe, but it was also meant to terrify. It was staged violence, pure and simple, and she didn't know what frightened her more—the fact of what it was or that part of her enjoyed it.

A jet of Bianca's blood wrapped around one of Zelandra's ebony ropes. The two slithered and snapped like snakes battling for their lives. A vine ensnared both before a spear of glass punctured the tangled mess, forcing the colors apart. Beyond the broken battle, Cindell's gaze asked silent questions. The breaking had been too easy. Bonds were meant to keep things together, not to be broken, and not to be broken by glass. With a wave of one hand, Cindell sent a glass spear toward Zelandra.

Zelandra's heart thudded. She used a chain to swipe the spear aside and took a half-step back, one hand flying to her stomach. Cindell suspected something. A second spear formed and flew. Shifting its course was child's play, but ignoring the veiled threat behind the attacks took much more effort. This was a mistake. She'd disappeared and not provided a cover story adequate to allay Cindell's suspicions. Bianca tended toward thinking the better of people, and Ori never let things bother her. But Cindell … Cindell was hard and cold like the glass she controlled. She was the one with the darkest past, the most grudges to hold, and the greatest temper. Trying to fool her was a fool's errand.

But you are not a fool. The Master's voice, slippery and sinister, coiled around her ears. *Or are you?*

No. No, she was not. She flicked her wrist, and a length of rope uncoiled from her fingers, twisting and spiraling around dueling blood and vine to shoot straight for Cindell. The azure mistress's eyes widened, and she formed a delicate shield just as the rope reached her. The barrier shattered, but it stopped the rope from reaching its target. Cindell spared a beat to regain herself before glaring at Zelandra once more.

The fight was not over. It had just begun.

Good. The Master's voice held approval now, as much approval as it ever did, at least. *Show them your might. You are amazing, magnificent. Make them believe.*

Zelandra squared her shoulders. Her hair whipped into a frenzy, dancing around her and tickling the flesh of her neck. She was astonishing, fantastic. She was what the audience had come to see. This was why she performed—to astound them.

And astound them, she would. She raised her hands, palms facing forward, and sent a volley of chains into the place where powers clashed. The rattling jangle clanked against Cindell's glass and clinked as it wrapped around vine and blood. In a moment, the battlefield was no longer theirs. It was hers, all hers, and she whipped it to her design, batting crimson, azure, and jade aside like she never had before. With her power wrapped around each, she brought them back together in a whirlwind funnel. Faster and faster they spun until it was impossible even for her to tell where one began and the next ended. The rattling chains grew to a rumble like thunder, cracking like lightning, lashing like driving rain. Her curls danced in the storm. She belonged here. She was everything here. She was power. Slowly, she lifted her hands above her head, making the funnel rise with them. The narrow point at its base rose above her head, leaving empty air and a clear view of Cindell. The azure mistress was no longer suspicious or angry. Fear engulfed her now.

Good.

Zelandra flung her arms wide. With a rushing snap, the funnel burst apart. Glass and chain flew in every direction, drawing screams from the audience. Blood and thorn rained down like a storm of crimson and jade. The last drops cleared the air, and Zelandra surveyed the audience. Dropped jaws. Wide eyes. Adults, children …

Him.

Torrick.

With a paralyzing jolt, her bonds stilled. Torrick watched her from his place toward the back of the tent, and his obvious fear almost stopped her heart. What had she done? She'd let the audience control her. She'd let the Master control her. She'd bent right to his will, unleashing destruction with abandon. All because she wanted to impress.

Well, no more.

She lowered her hands. Her hair ceased its frantic dance. She met Torrick's gaze with all her heart in her eyes. That wasn't her—that wasn't who she was.

A beat of silence.

A fading of fear.

He nodded.

And the ring exploded.

Crimson, azure, and jade came together in a ferocious battle, ripping, tearing, snarling. Zelandra did not join. This was not the life she wanted. This was not who she wished to be. She would not fight. She would not amaze the crowd, even though part of her begged for their approval. Torrick approved. That meant more to her than any applause.

What are you doing? The Master's voice was in her ear again, but it was no longer the seductive purr of everything she wanted. Now, it was the ringing of a bell calling her toward something she couldn't let herself have. *This is the grand performance. Fight them.*

No. She would not.

No? His voice turned sharp. *You do not say no. This is my circus, my performance. Fight them.*

I will not. And he could not make her. Through an opening in the scrabbling colors, she found Torrick's gaze again. She poured all her desperation into the contact, hoping and praying he understood.

He nodded once, stood, and moved to the back of the tent, prepared to run.

It was all she could do now to wait.

The battle continued. A jet of thorn detached from the fray and came for her. Zelandra batted it away, her hand again flying to her stomach.

Fight them, the Master snarled.

No.

Silence. *Then, be ready to suffer.*

Beneath her feet, the room shifted. The floor of the arena started to spin, the cue for the final shows of power. Bianca gathered blood to her and launched it into the air in a coiling, roiling cloud. Ori's thorns writhed and twisted in a battle all on their own. Cindell drew glass to her gown, making it shine, every inch a terrible queen.

Zelandra didn't move, just felt the floor move beneath her. Faster and faster until the audience blurred, and the world churned, and she could no longer find Torrick waiting to bring her to safety.

You cannot win. The Master's voice was so slow compared to the world whipping past her.

But she didn't need to win. She just needed to wait.

Faster, faster.

Crimson.

Azure.

Jade.

Goodbye.

The colors crashed together, swirling into a final show of power. With a flash, they were gone, and complete darkness settled. A beat of silence. And then the cheers. So many cheers.

A spotlight flickered to life above, illuminating Ori. She curtsied, her vines bowing with her. Zelandra used the light to find Torrick. He was gone, and she could only hope he ran fast enough.

The spotlight shifted to Cindell. She spread her glittering skirt and sank into a low bow. Next, Bianca curtsied, her crimson gown bold and beautiful beneath the light.

The light fell on Zelandra. The cheers grew louder. She bowed her head and closed her eyes. Torrick had to be almost free now.

You are weak. The Master's insult barely touched her. *I will show you how weak.*

She didn't listen. Didn't give him power. The cheers engulfed her, and she waited. Any moment now.

Bianca, Ori, and Cindell took one final bow.

Zelandra waited.

The spotlights winked out, plunging the tent into darkness. An invisible tether tugged at Zelandra as it always did after the performance, pulling her back to the Master's domain. Cindell, Ori, and Bianca glided backwards around her.

Zelandra didn't move.

What? Confusion and rage colored the Master's voice. *No, no. What have you done . . . ?*

What I had to do.

The tether broke away—even his bonds could not hold her. Another tether tugged at her from above, and Zelandra let it take her away from the Master and Grimmfay and the life she'd known for too long. She glanced back. Bianca and Ori watched her, their eyes wide and questioning. Zelandra's heart squeezed. They didn't deserve her betrayal, but she couldn't stay, not now that she knew what she missed. Far behind them, Cindell had already turned away and was moving fast, so fast.

But it didn't matter. Whatever the azure mistress did, she couldn't stop this, couldn't come between Zelandra and her freedom. Darkness, thick and absolute, surrounded her. She gave into its embrace one final time and let it bring her to the light.

Hansten

"Grenna." Yet again, his plea fell on unhearing ears. Grenna leaned forward, her attention fixed on the performance with frightening intensity. "Grenna, please."

She didn't glance his way, didn't even flinch.

Numbness settled in Hansten's chest. He was losing her. He was losing himself. Grenna's only reactions since the performance started had been for something in the ring. Every time, Hansten looked, and every time, it took him longer to pull his attention away. The mistresses were amazing. Amazing wasn't even a strong enough word. Their powers consumed his mind. The things they could do with glass and blood and thorns.

And Zelandra. He'd thought her show of manipulating rope

earlier had been fantastic, but it was nothing compared to what she did now. She was a dark storm surrounded by the glittering golden cloud of her hair snapping and writhing in a dance of its own. She stood tall, back arched and head held high, and he couldn't help but wonder if they were all lost.

Zelandra's green eyes swept over him like a physical force. She found something in the audience and jerked still. Then, suddenly, she was different. Still her, but not the tower fortress of a moment ago.

"What is she doing?" Grenna's voice was soft but sharp somehow.

"Grenna." Hansten leaned toward her. "Listen, we need—"

"That's not how it's supposed to go." Grenna glared at the performance ring.

Hansten blinked. "What?"

Zelandra had gone still like a statue. The other mistresses battled around her, tried to engage her, but Zelandra remained motionless. Her hair no longer danced. Instead, it seemed to gather around her like a blanket.

"She's wrong." Grenna's voice sent a shiver up Hansten's spine. There was more than his sister in the words. It was Grimmfay—it was the circus.

No. No! He wouldn't let it take her. It wouldn't have her. He was getting them out of here if he had to drag her kicking and screaming.

"Grenna." He gripped one of her small wrists and pulled her hand toward him.

She snapped to face him. "What are you doing?" She tugged her hand away.

Hansten tightened his hold. "Saving us." He fumbled with the length of chain Zelandra had given him, taking a few tries to drape it over Grenna's palm. "Hold this. You need to—"

"No!" Grenna jerked her arm, causing the chain to slip. She jerked again, and Hansten nearly lost his hold.

"Grenna, please." With frantic movements, Hansten tried and failed to lay the chain across Grenna's hand.

"No." Grenna's voice was a snarl.

Hansten held on to her struggling frame with all his strength, but he felt so small compared to her will. She fought him as if he meant to do her harm, as if he was the thing invading her being and trying to drag her toward the darkness. Didn't she see? The circus manipulated her. It lured her with beauty and promises, but it was false—all of it was false. Couldn't she feel the wrongness of it?

"Let go of me." Grenna yanked her arm out of his grasp.

Hansten reached for her and froze as brilliant light flashed. He squeezed his eyes shut. What was happening? The light faded, and specks danced behind his eyelids. There was a moment of silence, and then applause like thunder shook the air.

A spotlight illuminated each mistress for a bow. They glittered and glowed in their terrible glory. All but Zelandra, who simply lowered her head. Had she given up? Were they doomed?

The lights winked out. In the darkness, something latched on to Hansten like a tether around his heart. It tugged him upwards. Ahead, even in the near-pitch, he saw Zelandra floating toward him while the other mistresses were dragged back.

This was it. "Grenna." He gripped her shoulder with one hand and dangled the chain beside her with the other. "Grenna, grab ahold. We're free—we're leaving."

Slowly, Grenna turned to face him. It was her face, but there was something else in her expression, something cold and calculating and not his sister at all.

"No." Despite the cheers and applause, her voice reached his ears loud and clear. With strength greater than what she possessed, she shoved his hand away and turned back to the performance ring.

What? "Grenna!"

She didn't turn.

"Grenna!" He reached, but his hand closed around nothing. The tether pulled him backward, away from Grenna and Grimmfay and his last chance to free his baby sister from the monster. "Grenna, come on! Grenna!" His voice sounded muffled. He screamed louder, called her name with all the desperation in his heart.

She didn't move.

Darkness crowded in on him, and the roaring applause faded to nothing. Grenna … he couldn't leave her. He reached, but she was so far, getting farther. He kept his gaze locked on her, on the curve of her hair until it was too dark to see.

Until she was gone.

No. He tried to fight whatever force pulled him, but it was no use. He shot backward, faster and faster. Back, up, through something.

And then, light.

With a jolt, the force stopped. Hansten stumbled and caught

his balance, bracing his hands on his knees. Cool air—morning air—puffed past his face. It couldn't be. He straightened. The sky stretched overhead. To the east, light gathered on the horizon. Dawn approached. He was outside.

"Grenna?"

Nothing.

"Grenna?"

"Zel!" a man's voice called nearby.

Someone rushed past Hansten, nearly knocking him over. Again, Hansten stumbled and caught himself. The man rushed to a figure who lay a few feet away. "Zel, thank the Goddess." The man helped the figure—Zelandra—to her feet. She brushed her long hair back from her face and flung herself into his arms. Their lips met.

The comfort of Zelandra's presence lasted less than a second before the truth invaded. Grenna wasn't here. She'd pushed him away, chosen the circus. Tears welled and overflowed, and Hansten sank to his knees, some kind of animal sound escaping him.

"Hansten." It was Zelandra. She was at his side, wrapping her arms around him. "What happened? Where's your sister?"

Hansten couldn't answer. He collapsed into her embrace and sobbed. His sister was gone. Grenna had been taken by the darkness, the wrongness. She'd gone to it, wanted it. And there had been nothing he could do.

Sometime later, his tears slowed. Finally, his shoulders stopped heaving, and he sat up, wiping his lingering tears away. "She's ..." He sniffed. "She's gone."

Zelandra's hold tightened, but she didn't speak. What was there to say? Sorry wasn't near enough for what he felt, and she seemed to know it, understood somehow that the pain of losing someone to the circus was worse than any other kind of pain or loss.

"We should go," the man said after a long silence.

Hansten didn't move, and neither did Zelandra. Finally, she loosened her embrace a fraction. "Torrick is right."

Hansten blinked. "Torrick? Prince Torrick?" He extracted himself from Zelandra's arms and stood. Sure enough, the prince—unforgettable from the two times Hansten had seen him on visits to the city—was there. He gazed at something behind Hansten, his brow furrowed.

Hansten brushed grass from his tunic and turned, finding himself face-to-face with Grimmfay.

His breath caught. The circus seemed so small now. It had felt enormous while he was on its grounds, but now, it was as if all the majesty had been drained from its colors.

"It's so much smaller than I imagined." Zelandra sounded lost. She gathered her hair into a bundle at her chest, and a shudder passed through her. Her face bore no expression, but the longing in her eyes spoke volumes. Part of her wanted to go back, maybe would always want to go back.

He knew because part of him felt the pull. The child he'd been a few years ago urged him to run to the gates and force them open, take his chance to live among the wonder before it was too late.

To find Grenna and be with her forever.

He wanted to. Goddess, he wanted to.

But he couldn't.

The first rays of sunlight poked over the horizon, warming his skin. With them, Grimmfay faded. It seemed to both shrink in on itself and evaporate into mist. Hansten blinked, and in that one moment, a fraction of a second, the circus disappeared.

"Goodbye." Zelandra spoke so softly, but like Grenna's final word, this one reached his ears clearly.

Hansten watched the empty place where Grimmfay had been. It had taken his sister, but it wouldn't keep her. If it took his entire life, he would hunt down Grimmfay and force it to give back what it stole.

Grenna

What do you want it to be?

Grenna closed her eyes. She wanted a place for children to see and taste all the sweets Grimmfay offered. The pastries and candy and desserts were meant to be part of the show, not just something eaten between other shows.

She pictured a kitchen, her mother's kitchen, but unlike her mother, she didn't slave over a stove. She had helpers, lots of helpers. And they didn't make boring grains and berries or the occasional chicken. They made cakes and pies and breads. Candy bars and buns and chocolates of all kinds. And they did it surrounded by all kinds of goodies. They covered every bit of counter space, the table. The shelves along the walls.

Why not the walls themselves?

Because walls couldn't be candy.

Can't they?

She started to argue but stopped. Why couldn't they? Just because her house didn't have candy walls, didn't mean this house couldn't. This house was at the circus, where anything was possible.

Candy walls. And a dark chocolate floor. And a chimney of red and white like the cane-shaped candies they got from the city for holidays.

That's it. See it.

She saw it.

Wish it.

She wished. She wished so hard. She wished on the circus for her dream.

And though she didn't know it yet, a wish on the circus would come true, if not always in the way expected.

She opened her eyes and gasped.

Acknowledgements

Writing has been such a strange journey for me the last few years. After honestly thinking I'd given up on it for good, it's thrilling and terrifying to be at it again, and I can't thank my support team enough for just being there while I worked it out.

A big, huge thanks to Andie for reading this (and most of everything for Grimmfay) in its earliest form. Your insights are invaluable to making this world and its characters bolder and better. Also, your dead-pan delivery just cracks me up.

A megaphone-worthy cheer to my few but mighty patrons for your support as I timidly introduced my writing to the internet. In the deepest part of my heart, I suspected that going it on Patreon as a newbie wasn't necessarily the thing to do, but having that safe space gave me the courage to throw my hat back in the publishing ring, and I couldn't have done it without you.

I also need to thank the lovely group of women writers of Facebook for overwhelmingly voting on this title. Before this, it was "The Divide," which just did not have the magic of the circus. Seeing the overwhelming numbers for Once Upon a Broken Sky made that title fit this story.

And a special thanks to my Twitter worms. I found you while I was drafting Broken Sky, and having a community on Twitter, however small, has made trying to figure out social media so much less daunting. You've also just grown into a group I'm so thankful to be a part of, and when I said "watch me write a worm into my current book," who knew that would actually be such a pivotal moment of the story?

To my parents for introducing me to fantasy fiction. I'd apologize for what me reading Terry Goodkind at the tender age of 12 probably did to your nerves, but it started me down this path, so I can't say I'm too sorry. Even if I just stopped having nightmares about that scene from Temple of the Winds.

And no acknowledgements section would be complete without Dave, the best partner a girl could ask for, and my Little Fish. For dealing with me going off somewhere in my head while my plot resolves itself, for getting me through my last few years of "I'm tired of writing and being told I'm not good enough," for believing in me when I refused to believe in myself—there are no words but thank you, and I love you both so much.

About M.T. DeSantis

Born a New Englander, M.T. DeSantis moved south in early adulthood, realized she actually liked winter, and promptly moved back north. She's currently trying out life as a Michigander/anian with her family, who also (mostly) actually like winter. When not making word magic, M.T. can be found practicing yoga, attempting to make friends with the oven, or trying to read while people keep talking to her. For updates, fun emails, and a free story from the world of Grimmfay, join her newsletter at https://bf.kitnkabookle.com/seeing-pool

The tale of the dark and mysterious circus continues in Grimmfay. Visit bf.kitnkabookle.com/grimmfay for a free story from the circus and to join M.T.'s author newsletter for updates and notifications of new books.

One more, no matter what must be done, there shall be...

Twelve years ago, Queen Zelandra escaped Grimmfay's hold on her soul, leaving a vengeful circus in her wake. Now, Grimmfay has returned to reclaim what it lost, and it will not leave without its fourth mistress. Barricaded in her palace, Zelandra will do anything to fight the siren call threatening to drag her back.

But Grimmfay has not come for her. It's come for her daughter. Told from alternating perspectives, all with a different view of the circus, Grimmfay is a story of the enemies we face, the sides we choose, and the battles we must fight, even when we're not sure we can win. Come one, come any to the place where wishes are granted and dreams come true...but not always in the way expected.

www.ingramcontent.com/pod-product-compliance
Lightning Source LLC
LaVergne TN
LVHW051007080826
845145LV00009B/2501

* 9 7 8 1 9 6 2 8 3 8 0 1 6 *